TO HATCH A THIEF

TO HATCH A THIEF

A MOVIE CLUB MYSTERIES NOVELLA

ZARA KEANE

BEAVERSTONE PRESS LLC

Published by Beaverstone Press GmbH (LLC)

Paperback ISBN: 978-3-90624-552-2

A NOTE ON GAELIC TERMS

Certain Gaelic terms appear in this book. I have tried to use them sparingly and in contexts that should make their meaning clear to international readers. However, a couple of words require clarification.

The official name for the Irish police force is *An Garda Síochána* ("the Guardian of the Peace"). Police are *Gardaí* (plural) and *Garda* (singular). Irish police are commonly referred to as "the guards".

The official rank of a police officer such as Sergeant O'Shea is Garda Sergeant O'Shea. As the Irish frequently shorten this to Sergeant, I've chosen to use this version for all but the initial introduction to the character.

The official name for the Whisper Island police station would be Whisper Island Garda Station, but Maggie, being American, rarely thinks of it as such.

The Irish police do not, as a rule, carry firearms.

Permission to carry a gun is reserved to detectives and specialist units, such as the Emergency Response Unit. The police on Whisper Island would not have been issued with firearms.

Although this book follows American spelling conventions, I've chosen to use the common Irish spelling for proper names such as Carraig Harbour and the Whisper Island Medical Centre. An exception is the Movie Theater Café, which was named by Maggie's American mother.

Five weeks ago, I'd given my cheating ex and crumbling career in the San Francisco PD the proverbial middle finger, and moved to the Wild West...of Ireland. In that time, I'd learned to bake scones without burning them (okay, I still scrape off scorch marks), rescued a kitten trapped in a drainpipe (well, I'd helped), and solved a murder (that one really was me). All things considered, my time on Whisper Island hadn't been the restful vacation my aunt Noreen had promised, but I'd had a blast.

On the Tuesday after I'd caught a killer, I schlepped a tray laden with blueberry muffins from the kitchen of the Movie Theater Café. I dumped it on the counter and wiped the back of my hand over my damp brow. "Man, that's heavy. Are you planning to force-feed your customers, Noreen?" I waved an arm around the half-empty café. "We'll never sell all of these muffins before closing time."

My aunt regarded me over the rim of her spectacles. "They're for the school bake sale, love. I told you about it yesterday evening, but you had your nose stuck in one of Mammy's old magazines."

I brightened at the mention of my late grandmother's collection of vintage movie magazines. "They were awesome. It was like stepping back in time to the days of Old Hollywood."

"Mammy's magazine collection is huge," Noreen said while adding milk froth to a cappuccino. "Philomena is storing them at her house. Ask her to let you borrow more."

"I will. My only hesitation is in handling the oldest issues. They must be worth a chunk of change."

"John thinks we should sell them on eBay." Noreen snorted, emphasizing her disdain for her brother-in-law's outrageous suggestion. "Typical man. If we'd discovered a stack of old car magazines, he'd be all over them."

"Very true. Where did Granny find all of her movie magazines? A few in her collection are American. *Modern Screen*, for example. Were they sold outside the U.S.?"

"I'm not sure," my aunt mused, "but I know Mammy got her copies from a friend who moved to Boston. They both loved the cinema, and they used to send each other magazines as a way to keep in touch over the years."

"How sweet. It was almost worth getting the flu to have a chance to read Granny's magazine collection." As if on cue, I sneezed, and rooted in my apron pocket for a tissue.

My aunt shook her head and gave me a reproving look. "I told you to stay in bed today."

"I'm feeling much better," I said in a voice that would have been ideal had I had a penchant for making pervy phone calls. "Honestly. And I'm covering my hands with disinfectant every five seconds."

My aunt clucked in disapproval. "After your adventure chasing a killer, I'm not surprised you got sick. You've been running yourself ragged since you arrived on Whisper Island. Take this as a sign that you need to slow down and take a break."

I gave a wry smile. "Taking a break isn't one of my strengths. I like to be busy."

"Being busy is all very well, but I don't want you infecting my customers." With this statement, Noreen put the cappuccino on a tray next to an espresso and two berry scones, and bustled over to Bette Davis, one of the movie star-themed tables that were in keeping with the theme of a café housed in a renovated movie theater.

My phone vibrated with an incoming message. I slipped it out of my pocket and glanced at the display. I stared at the words on the screen and drew my brows together.

Maggie, would you please come by my office today? Or tell me a time and place we could meet? I'd appreciate your advice on a delicate matter, and I need you to be discreet. Regards, Jennifer Pearce

Why on earth did Jennifer Pearce, of all people, need *my* help? I'd met the uptight lawyer during the murder case, but we weren't exactly besties. She was the last person I'd have expected to reach out to me in a crisis. On the other hand, I owed her a favor, and I always paid my debts. While my aunt served coffees and took more customer orders, I typed a quick reply.

Hey, Jennifer. Sure. I'll swing by your place during my break. Say two-thirty? See you then. Maggie

After I'd hit send, I poured myself a glass of water and attempted to swallow two painkillers without my aunt seeing me. From across the room, Noreen's eagle eye caught me in the act. "Go home, Maggie," she barked. "Sister Pauline agrees with me. Don't you, sister?"

This remark was addressed to my aunt's good friend, and my cohort in a recent boat chase, Sister Pauline McLoughlin. In addition to her work at the church, the nun taught part-time at Whisper Island's elementary school. I'd gotten to know her during my short time on the island and considered her a friend. This was borne out by her next words.

"Stop bossing Maggie around, Noreen. She's old

enough to know what's best for her." The nun fixed me with a steely gaze. "Which is why she's going to be sensible and go to bed."

Gee, thanks, pal. I pulled a face. "Oh, all right. You've nagged me into submission."

If I were honest, coming to work today *had* been a lousy idea. Although my fever was gone, my headache and sore throat were not. But it was either drag my carcass to the café or stay in a bed shared with Roly, Poly, and their feline offspring. Until my new place was habitable, I was sharing Noreen's cramped cottage with her eight cats (not counting the kittens), a wild puppy, and a menagerie of animals from her petting zoo. I loved my aunt dearly, but I was itching for my space.

My aunt returned to the counter and packed the muffins I'd brought out from the kitchen into two large plastic containers. "Can you do me a favor and drop these off at the school on your way home?"

"Su—*ure.*" Another sneeze sliced the word in two. Yeah, I needed sleep, with or without a cat-infested bed.

"I'll put some of my chicken broth into a container for you, and you can warm it up at home." Noreen grabbed a soup container from beneath the counter. "You need feeding."

The last thing I felt like was food. "There's no need—"

"There's every need. You have to be fit for the dance on Saturday."

I slow-blinked. "Dance?" I croaked. "What dance?"

"The annual Valentine's Day dance at the town hall." Noreen beamed at me. "Paddy Driscoll is looking forward to taking you for a spin."

"Somehow, I highly doubt your grumpy neighbor wants me anywhere near him. He's still sore about the dog getting in with his sheep."

"Sure, Bran wouldn't hurt a fly. The sheep came to no harm." Noreen waved her hand in a dismissive gesture. "Paddy's not a people person. He'll get used to you after a while."

My lips twitched. "After I've lived on the island for twenty-five years?"

My aunt's expression grew smug. "See? I knew you'd decide to stay."

"Hey, I didn't say that. I've agreed to stay until the end of May, and then I'll reassess the situation."

Noreen headed for the kitchen. "Once you settle into your new home," she said over her shoulder, "you'll never want to leave. Sure, those new holiday cottages are gorgeous."

As a thank-you to me for solving the murder case, Noreen and several other islanders had pooled their resources and paid the rent on a holiday home for a couple of months. The cottage was currently undergoing renovations, but I'd be able to move in by the end of February.

"We'll see," I said in a noncommittal tone. I was tempted to extend my stay on Whisper Island until the end of the summer, but I wanted to wait and see how I felt closer to the time. My gut told me to stay, but after the emotional roller coaster of my separation, I didn't trust my instincts to make the right decision.

Noreen returned with a container filled with chicken soup. She sealed the lids of the muffin boxes and handed me the pile of containers. "I'll send Julie a text to meet you outside the school in ten minutes. Sound good?"

I checked my watch. Two-ten. A little early for my appointment with Jennifer Pearce, but I wouldn't make it back on time if I swung by the elementary school first. "Can you tell Julie I'll be there in forty-five minutes? I have an errand to run first."

"Okay." My aunt pulled out her phone and typed a message to my cousin.

"Are you sure you don't mind me borrowing your car again?" I asked. "I feel bad about constantly leaving you carless."

Noreen glanced up. "Not at all. I can get a lift home with someone when I close the café. But if you're staying on the island, you'll need a set of wheels under you. Try Kerrigan Motors on the mainland. They have an excellent reputation for used cars."

"Wait...what about the Knitting Club meeting? I'm supposed to serve tonight." As a way to supplement her income, my aunt allowed various island clubs and special interest societies to use the café in the evenings. In return, the clubs agreed to buy food and drink from the café.

"Don't worry about it. Philomena and I will manage just fine. Go home and get some sleep."

"Okay. Will do." I waved goodbye to my aunt and the café customers and stepped out onto the sidewalk.

A gale force wind nearly blew me off my feet. I struggled to the car with my load and piled the boxes neatly onto the floor of the passenger side and locked the car. I'd leave the car here and walk the short distance to Jennifer Pearce's office.

Nesbitt & Son Solicitors was located on Lynott Lane, a side street off Greer Street, the main thoroughfare through Smuggler's Cove. It took me five minutes to walk from the car to the corner of Lynott Lane.

When I turned into the lane, I froze in my tracks. A crowd had gathered in front of Jennifer's office building. Everyone gawked at the police car that was parked haphazardly on the sidewalk, blue lights flashing. Sean Clough, the editor of the *Whisper Island Gazette* and next-door neighbor to Nesbitt & Son, nodded a greeting before returning his attention to the unfolding spectacle.

Before I could marshal my thoughts, the door to the lawyers' practice swung open and Garda Sergeant

O'Shea led Jennifer Pearce down the steps to the waiting police vehicle. As always, Jennifer was impeccably groomed in a sleek pencil skirt, blazer, and blouse, but the stray wisps of dark hair escaping from her elaborate up-do betrayed a chink in her armor. From the police sergeant's body language and the lawyer's chalky complexion, I knew this wasn't a matter of Jennifer being asked to represent one of her clients during a police interrogation.

A moment later, Aaron Nesbitt, Jennifer's boss, erupted out of the building, his cheeks blazing red. "This is utterly outrageous. Jennifer would never—"

His coworker's warning look silenced the older lawyer, and Aaron Nesbitt's words stuttered to a halt.

The newspaper editor peppered Sergeant O'Shea with questions, but his efforts were rewarded with a brusque, "No comment."

Before she got into the police car, Jennifer's gaze moved in my direction. My eyes met hers, and I read fear and desperation in their depths. She gave a slight shake of her head. I got the message: say nothing and wait.

Ignoring the newspaper editor's barrage of follow-up questions, O'Shea closed the back door behind Jennifer, slid behind the wheel, and took off.

I stared at the space where the police car had been long after they'd left. Whatever Jennifer had wanted me to be discreet about, I had the feeling the cat was well and truly out of the bag.

2

Ten minutes and twenty sneezes after Jennifer Pearce's dramatic exit in a squad car, I pulled up in front of Whisper Island's only elementary school.

As promised, Julie was waiting to unburden me of my load. I got out of the car, and my cousin recoiled at the sight of me.

"Wow, Maggie. You look like death."

"Thanks for the compliment," I said dryly.

"Seriously, you should be in bed."

"So people keep telling me." After removing two enormous muffins from one of the containers, I scooped up the boxes and handed them to my cousin. "That's everything. Unless you want the invalid soup Noreen is trying to persuade me to drink?"

Julie laughed. "I'll pass. Thanks so much for dropping off the muffins."

"No problem." I shifted my weight from one leg to the other, unsure whether to mention the Jennifer Pearce incident. *Well*, I mused, *she'll find out sooner or later*. On Whisper Island, gossip spread faster than the flu. "Do you know why the police would want to speak to Jennifer Pearce?"

My cousin frowned. "Jennifer? Is it legal business?"

"Put it this way: it didn't look like Sergeant O'Shea was consulting her in her professional capacity."

Julie's bewildered expression increased. "I can't imagine Jennifer being involved with anything dodgy. She's too uptight for that."

"That's what I think." When I turned to get back into the car, a thought struck me. "Hey, have you been roped into going to a dance on Saturday?"

My cousin shuddered. "Gosh, yes. The Valentine's Day dance is an annual and much-beloved island event. Beloved, that is, by all but me."

I cocked an eyebrow. "That bad?"

"It's awful," she said with feeling. "Think of a bunch of hermit farmers poured into their one good suit and trotted out for their annual attempt to socialize."

I snorted with laughter. "Noreen mentioned that my good pal, Paddy Driscoll, would be attending."

Julie nodded. "Paddy always goes. And Mum and Noreen always push him to dance with me. He's surprisingly light on his feet actually."

11

"If he's that good of a dancer, Noreen should dance with him herself."

"Oh, she does." My cousin grinned. "I suspect she has a crush on him."

My jaw dropped. "No way."

"Yes way. Mum says they used to go out together, but Paddy never had the guts to propose."

"Interesting." I filed this information away for future contemplation. I'd never considered why Noreen had never married, and I couldn't imagine her out on a date.

"Anyway, thanks for dropping off the muffins." My cousin regarded me dubiously. "Will you be well enough for Friday's Movie Club meeting?"

"Definitely," I said, emphasizing the point with a massive sneeze. "We're watching Cary Grant in *To Catch a Thief*. It's one of my favorites."

"Promise me you'll only come if you're well enough."

"Pinky swear." I gestured toward the school entrance. "Now go make the kids happy with those muffins."

My cousin laughed. "They're supposed to be selling them, not eating them."

I grinned. "Good luck with that."

When I climbed back into the car, I checked the clock on the dashboard. I'd swing by the station and try to bribe whoever was on desk duty into being indiscreet. My gaze strayed to the two muffins I'd sprung from the bake sale goodies. Bribery in the form of baked goods would be my weapon.

February was still low season on Whisper Island, and the afternoon traffic was light. A few minutes after leaving the school, I reached the Whisper Island Garda Station. When I pulled into the station's parking lot, Sergeant Liam Reynolds was climbing off his Harley, dressed in civvies.

Muttering under my breath, I grabbed the muffins and got out of the car. Our gazes clashed. A by-now-familiar prickle of heat spread across my skin. "Sergeant," I said, or rather, croaked.

"Ms. Doyle." His lips twitched with amusement. "I should have known you'd show up. Drawn to trouble, as per usual."

My eyes widened, and my attention flew to the door of the solicitor's practice. "Jennifer."

"Yeah." He cocked his head to the side and grinned at me. "Your pal is in a bucket load of hot water."

"She's not exactly my pal."

"Yet here you are, running to her rescue." He dropped his gaze. "With muffins."

"How do you know I'm here to help Jennifer?" I demanded in a haughty tone.

"I doubt you're here to visit Sergeant O'Shea," Reynolds said cheerfully, "unless those muffins contain strychnine."

"Nope. I was hoping to bribe whatever dork of a reserve garda was stuck on desk duty."

Reynolds's deep chuckle brought heat to my cheeks. "Not a reserve, but I'm on desk duty this afternoon. I guess those muffins are for me." He swiped one out of my hand before I could protest, and took a bite. "Delicious. I guess you didn't bake them."

"I'll have you know my baking skills are improving," I said in a tone of outrage. Okay, 'improving' was pushing it, but the smoke alarm hadn't gone off in an entire week. I considered this progress.

Reynolds turned on his heel and strode toward the entrance, forcing me to jog to keep pace with his long strides. "I was expecting you. Aaron Nesbitt told me you'd show up."

"Did he now? And how would he know that? Has he developed clairvoyant tendencies?"

"Apparently, Jennifer wanted to consult you about a client, and she mentioned it to Aaron."

"Yeah, she texted me to arrange a meeting, but she didn't say what she wanted to talk to me about."

Reynolds shoved open the station door and gestured for me to enter. When we were inside, he swung his backpack behind the front desk. "I can guess that whatever Jennifer wanted to discuss with you is connected with the reason she was brought in for questioning. Take a seat while I put on my uniform."

I obeyed and chose the least uncomfortable of the police station's hard plastic chairs. I picked up a tattered magazine from the pile on the coffee table and leafed through it absently, barely seeing the pictures or words before me. What could Jennifer have done to warrant such a dramatic entrance from the notoriously lazy Sergeant O'Shea? The older police officer was usually more concerned with his next round of golf than with maintaining law and order on Whisper Island.

Reynolds reappeared after a few minutes, looking disturbingly handsome in his uniform. "Can I offer you a coffee?"

I wrinkled my nose. "Thanks, but no thanks. I value my stomach lining."

He laughed. "Our machine isn't up to the high standards set by the Movie Theater Café, that's for sure."

"A glass of water would be good."

"Sure." Reynolds filled a large glass with mineral water and handed it to me. "You don't look too hot today. Did the flu get you?"

I pulled a face and nodded. "I'm going back to bed once I've spoken to Jennifer."

Reynolds jerked a thumb in the direction of the station's only interrogation room. "That might take a while. I popped my head round the door a moment ago, and it looked like O'Shea was just warming up."

"Why's he handling the questioning and not you? I thought you were supposed to be in charge."

Reynolds's grin widened. "Officially, I'm helping

him to wind down toward retirement. Today is my day off, but with Sergeant O'Shea busy, and neither of the reserves available, I came in to cover the phones and anything else that crops up."

"So..." I lowered my voice. "Why the coffee? You've got to have an ulterior motive for being nice to me."

He schooled his features into an expression of faux hurt. "Maybe I'm just being nice to my future neighbor."

"Hmm...maybe, but I don't buy it. Why are you so keen to talk to me?"

Reynolds glanced in the direction of the interrogation room. "Because I know what Jennifer wanted to talk to you about, and why."

"Well, go on," I demanded, leaning forward. "Don't leave me in suspense."

"Jennifer has been accused of stealing a valuable diamond necklace that belongs to a client."

I drew back and stared at him, slack-jawed. "'Jennifer' and 'stealing' don't belong in the same sentence. You've met the woman. She takes herself and her job way too seriously to jeopardize it by stealing from a client."

Reynolds shrugged. "Nevertheless, the client—or rather, the client's heirs—are adamant that Jennifer took the necklace."

"Okay, tell me the whole story. I'm intrigued."

"It's not my case..." he trailed off, leaving me to fill in the blank.

"Not yet." I grinned. "Go on."

"Jennifer and Aaron are handling the estate of a client who died in a nursing home on Whisper Island a few months ago. The man's heirs have been fighting over their inheritance since the funeral. They thought that Matt Malone, the dead guy, was dirt poor, but it turns out he had a pile of cash stashed away under the floorboards—literally. As well as the cash, Malone owned valuable diamond necklaces. I don't know the full details, but that's what I gleaned from O'Shea."

"Where did the money and the jewels come from?"

"Gambling. Apparently, Malone was a gifted poker player."

"Poker is legal in Ireland, right?" I frowned. "I think I read that somewhere."

Reynolds nodded. "As long as the game adheres to certain rules, and Malone always made sure to avoid illegal poker games.

"If people knew Malone was a talented gambler," I mused, "why were they surprised to discover he had money?"

"His friends say he played to win, but he wasn't interested in the winnings. He was content with his life on the island and saw no reason to change it. Malone won most of his big prize money off the island, so people around here didn't necessarily know how much cash he'd won."

"What about the tax folks?" I asked. "Did they know about it?"

"Yes. Malone declared his winnings on his tax forms. It was all above board, even his decision to keep cash in his house. No one is obliged to keep their wealth in a bank."

"So Malone's friends knew he had cash lying around, even if they weren't aware how much?"

Reynolds shook his head. "No. Malone made no secret of his distrust of banks, especially after the Irish banking crisis, but he wasn't a fool. The only people who knew he kept cash in his house were his lawyers."

I digested this information for a moment before saying, "Tell me more about the necklace."

Reynolds slid another glance at the closed door. "As I said, Malone stored his winnings under the floorboards. I'm not sure of the exact details, but he left instructions in his will with a list of the various locations he'd hidden his wealth. Among the loot was the diamond necklace that Jennifer Pearce is accused of stealing."

"Who made the accusation?"

"Matt Malone's sons. It looks bad for Aaron and Jennifer because they failed to report the break-in to us."

I nodded. "Okay. Go on with the story."

"As I said, Malone had a deep distrust of banks. His instructions were that Nesbitt & Son should collect his loot from his house after his death and store it in their safe until probate was over."

I whistled. "That's a heck of a risk."

"Aaron and Jennifer weren't comfortable with this stipulation, but they were being paid a hefty fee for their services. Malone's four children were scattered around the globe, and no one else knew about the contents of the safe." Reynolds's smile was wry. "At least, no one officially knew, apart from Aaron, Jennifer, and Matt Malone's heirs."

"Which is why when the diamond necklace was discovered to be missing, the fickle finger of suspicion pointed at Jennifer," I finished.

"Yeah." Reynolds flexed his shoulders. "The whole business stinks."

"Your esteemed colleague doesn't seem to think so."

"Sergeant O'Shea doesn't have much experience dealing with thefts on this scale," Reynolds said, determinedly diplomatic about his waste-of-space fellow police officer.

"Where do I come into the picture?" I asked. "There has to be a reason you're telling me all this."

"When Jennifer gets out of here—which she will in another hour or two—my guess is that she's going to ask you to do some discreet digging on her behalf." Reynolds chuckled. "I'd like you to refuse."

"What?" I shot out of my seat. "No way."

"Sh." Reynolds held a finger over his lips. "You don't want Sergeant O'Shea coming out here and seeing you."

With a reluctant grunt, I slumped back onto my seat. "Why tell me all of this and then turn around and warn me not to get involved?"

"First off, you're sick. The smartest thing for you to do is to go home and sleep. And second, I haven't known you long, but I can guess you'll leap at the opportunity to go haring off in pursuit of the thief." The laughter lines around Reynolds's eyes deepened. "I'm politely asking you not to stick your nose in this case. I fully intend to be put in charge of the investigation—" the unspoken implication that it would be with or without O'Shea's cooperation hung in the air, "—and I don't want you involved."

"Charming." I crossed my arms over my chest. "I helped you catch a killer last week."

"For which I'm very grateful, but that is to be your only foray into cracking crimes in Ireland. Do we understand one another?"

I sniffed. "Perfectly."

He beamed. "Excellent. Then you promise to stay out of this?"

"What can a woman with the flu add to your stellar detective skills, Sergeant?" I stood up and allowed a slow smile to spread across my face, enjoying the flicker of uncertainty in his deep blue eyes. "I'll go home to my chicken soup and leave you to solve the crime."

"Maggie, I'm serious," he called after me as I swept out of the police station.

I looked back at him over my shoulder, savoring the sight of the handsome police officer looking flustered. "So am I, Sergeant. So am I."

3

*M*y next stop was at McConnell's Pharmacy, where I threw myself at the mercy of my friend Mack. "I need a cure for the flu."

"Don't we all." Mack cast a look of longing at the back room in which he kept his lab equipment. "If I invent a cure for influenza, I'll make my fortune."

"Until you go down in the annals of pharmaceutical history, do you at least have something that'll mask my symptoms?"

The pharmacist looked me over and shook his head. "Are you sure you have the flu? If you had the real deal, you wouldn't be able to move."

"Flu, bad cold, whatever. What can I take that doesn't need a script?"

"A what?" Mack blinked for a moment. "Oh, you mean a doctor's prescription. As well as making sure you get plenty of rest and liquids, you could try Day and Night Nurse." He took a couple of packages from a shelf and turned back to me. "I recommend the Day Nurse capsules for during the day, and the Night Nurse in liquid form for the night."

"As long as they work and don't knock me on my behind, I'm happy."

"Don't you want to know the ingredients?" Mack frowned at me as though I were an inattentive student.

I sighed. "No, but I get the impression that you won't sell them to me unless I let you give me a chemistry lecture."

He laughed and rattled off a list of ingredients, some of which sounded familiar. I slapped a few notes on the counter and grabbed my meds. "Thanks, Mack. I'll see you at the Movie Club on Friday."

A line appeared between Mack's brows. "Will you be well enough to go?"

"If your medicines are as effective as you say, sure I will." I gave him a mock salute and sauntered out of the pharmacy.

Back in the car, I opened the package of Day Nurse. After a cursory glance at the instructions, I popped a pill and downed it with the bottle of mineral water I always carried in my purse. Now that I was medicated, it was time to get to work. While I had Jennifer Pearce's number stored on my phone, I didn't have Aaron Nesbitt's. I opened my phone's browser and looked up Nesbitt & Son. I hit the number that popped up on my screen. Aaron answered on the second ring.

"Ms. Doyle," he said after I'd introduced myself, "I'm glad you called. Would it be possible for you to meet me this afternoon?"

"Sure. I'll swing by your place now. I'm parked on the main street, so I'll be there in a sec."

"Thank you." The man's relief was palpable.

I slipped my phone back in my purse and got out of the car for what felt like the hundredth time that afternoon. There had to be more to this story than Reynolds had revealed, I thought as I retraced my steps from earlier to Lynott Lane. Why else would Jennifer and Aaron be so keen to involve an outsider like me instead of relying on the police?

A vision of that incompetent oaf, Sergeant O'Shea, danced before my eyes and I swallowed a snort. Maybe Aaron and Jennifer would feel more confident once Reynolds wrested the investigation out of O'Shea's grubby hands. The thought of O'Shea raised another pertinent question. Why was the notoriously work-shy police officer suddenly keen to take on this case? Something didn't add up.

In contrast to earlier, Lynott Lane was deserted, and no curious crowd loitered in front of the entrance to Nesbitt & Son Solicitors. I pressed the bell and Aaron's voice crackled over the intercom. "Ms. Doyle? I'll buzz you in."

Inside, a short flight of stairs led up to the first

landing. Aaron Nesbitt stood in the doorframe, waiting for me. He was around Noreen's age and wore his curly silver hair short. Like Jennifer, Aaron was impeccably dressed and looked as though he'd been transplanted from a big city law firm to this small two-person show on Whisper Island. However, I knew from my aunts that Aaron had inherited Nesbitt & Son from his father, and had practiced on Whisper Island since the day he'd qualified as a solicitor.

Ignoring my tiredness, I took the stairs two at a time and forced a confident smile. "Hello, Mr. Nesbitt." I stretched out an arm.

He shook my hand with a firm, confident shake. "Thank you for coming, Ms. Doyle. Please call me Aaron."

"Then I'm Maggie."

Aaron led me through a fusty reception area where an equally fusty assistant tapped away on a keyboard.

"Could you serve tea in my office, Mary?"

The woman glanced up and gave me a critical stare over her horn-rimmed glasses. Then her lined face lit up. "You're Noreen and Philomena's niece."

"Yeah. I'm Maggie." It still felt weird to be recognized by people I didn't know. I was used to the anonymity of living in a big city where strangers neither knew nor cared what I was called, or who my family was.

"I'm Mary Driscoll, Paddy's sister. I went to school

with your dad." The woman's broad smile lit up her homely face. "Dermot was always the class clown."

The idea that my dour father came from this warm, welcoming community still baffled me, and the notion that he'd once been the class clown was even more bewildering. Mary must have mixed him up with someone with a sense of humor.

I followed Aaron into his office, and he motioned for me to take a seat. I chose one of the sleek leather armchairs that faced Aaron's impossibly neat desk.

"How's Jennifer?" I asked. "I hoped to catch her at the station earlier, but she was in with Sergeant O'Shea."

Aaron's nostrils flared ever so slightly, betraying the anger that simmered beneath his cool and collected exterior. "That buffoon. Jennifer is bearing up. The police let her go half an hour ago, and I told her to go home. The stress brought on one of her migraines."

"At least she hasn't been charged with anything."

"Not *yet*," Aaron grunted. "Sergeant O'Shea wanted to keep her longer, but the new guy intervened."

"Sergeant Reynolds filled me in on some of the background," I began. "I assume that's why I'm here."

Aaron nodded. "Yes. Jennifer suggested we contact you. She felt your...professional experience...might prove useful."

"I'm not a cop over here," I cautioned. "I have no jurisdiction and no right to question people."

"I know. That's why you're perfect."

"Maybe you can expand on what Sergeant Reynolds told me."

Before Aaron could begin, Mary arrived with the tea tray. Normally, I preferred coffee, but my sore throat was grateful for a cup of hot tea today. After Mary had left, Aaron began his tale.

"Matt Malone was a family friend. He and my father were at school together, and they both came back to the island after university." Aaron took a sip of tea before continuing, weighing his next words carefully. "They were the only boys in their year to get college degrees. My father studied law and qualified as a solicitor, and Matt took a degree in mathematics. Everyone expected Matt to stay in academia, or qualify as a secondary school teacher, but he chose to come back to Whisper Island and take over the family farm. He married a local girl, had four children, and lived a mundane existence. The only unusual thing about the man was his love of poker."

"Did you know he had money?"

"Not until my father died and I took over as Matt's solicitor." Aaron gave a wry smile. "When I first read the terms of his will, I thought it was a joke. But when I saw the precise sums named, I stopped laughing. Matt Malone used to come in once a year for a consultation and to update the terms of his will. He wanted specific sums of money spelled out in the will, and they grew every year."

"I understand his cash and a necklace was in your safe?"

"Not exactly." Aaron sighed. "I never should have agreed to the scheme. Matt had an aversion to banks. I don't know why, and he never elaborated. He just refused to put his money into them. When I explained to him that my safe wasn't big enough to hold two million euros worth of five-hundred euro notes, Matt went out and bought four diamond necklaces, each worth half a million euros."

I whistled. "Wow."

"The idea was that the necklaces represented each of his children's inheritance." Aaron sighed. "And I was to keep all four in my safe during the period of probate. Matt paid for the insurance in advance, but no insurance will cover us if we're convicted of stealing from a client."

"Are all four necklaces missing?"

Aaron shook his head. "Just the one."

"And you're positive that neither you nor Jennifer took it?"

The man looked horrified. "Of course we didn't take it. I know I didn't, and I can't believe Jennifer would be capable of such a crime."

"What about your assistant? Does she have access to the safe?"

"No. Jennifer and I are the only ones with the code, and the only people who knew about the necklaces are me, Jennifer, and Matt Malone's children." He paused. "And anyone involved with the processing of probate, I suppose."

"Is your legal practice protected by an alarm when you're not here?"

"Yes, but not one that's connected to the police." Aaron tugged at his collar. "Until recently, Whisper Island has always been a very safe place to live."

"Okay, let's start with Matt Malone's children. Where are they now?"

Aaron frowned. "Let me see. Susan lives in Dublin with her family. Jane is in London. Enda immigrated to Australia, but he's staying with his brother, Mick, at the Whisper Island Hotel at the moment."

My ears pricked up at this information. "So both of Matt Malone's sons are currently on the island?"

"Yes, but I can't see either of them breaking into my office and robbing my safe."

"Maybe they wanted to increase their share of their father's estate."

"Perhaps, but this is a risky way to do it. It's not easy to convert a diamond necklace of that value into cash without the authorities getting wind of the scheme."

"And even if they did sell it on the black market, they'd be unlikely to get its full value." I considered this conundrum for a moment. Valuable jewelry was tough to shift, and a bad choice for a criminal looking to make a quick buck. "Why did O'Shea latch onto Jennifer as the culprit? Why not you?"

"Because Jennifer was the last person to handle the necklaces. On the request of one of Matt Malone's daughter's, she brought all of them to a jeweler in Galway last week to be formally appraised, but she swears she put all four necklaces back in the safe the moment she got back to the office. I believe her. Why risk her career for half a million euros? It might seem like a vast sum of money to many people, but Jennifer comes from a wealthy family, and she's engaged to a wealthy man. Why would she jeopardize everything for a necklace?"

Why indeed? I didn't have Jennifer down as a thief or an embezzler, but I'd be a fool to rule her out this early in the investigation. And I wasn't ruling Aaron out yet, either.

"If the necklaces were insured, I assume they'd already been valued by a professional. Why did Malone's daughter want it done again?"

"The Malone siblings aren't close. At least, the sisters don't speak to the brothers, and vice versa. Jane expressed concern that the four necklaces might not be of equal value, and she requested a second opinion on the necklaces' respective values."

"That sounds reasonable." I eyed Nesbitt carefully. "Do you have any idea why the Malone siblings dislike each other?"

"I don't know the precise ins and outs, but Jane mentioned one of her brothers cheating her out of her savings. Suffice it to say, there's no love lost between them." Aaron cast me a pleading look. "So will you help us? I don't trust Sergeant O'Shea, and you can ask questions where we can't. We'll pay you for your services, of course."

"I don't exactly hang out a shingle for my services, as you put it," I said dryly. "I'm an ex-cop who works at her aunt's café."

"You solved a murder. You caught the killer with your own hands."

That wasn't quite how the situation had gone down, but I didn't feel like going into the details.

"You're ideal to dig up dirt on Matt Malone's children, and anyone else who might have known about the necklaces," Aaron continued. "We want to hire you to be our unofficial private eye."

4

On Wednesday morning, my plan to begin my
investigation into the disappearance of the
diamond necklace was derailed by a high fever. So
much for Mack's medicines. I groaned and rolled over
in my bed, and then groaned some more when the
room spun around me in drunken waves. The day
passed in a feverish blur. I was vaguely aware of
Noreen bringing me soup and something to drink, and
I recalled Poly staring resentfully at me for taking up
too much space in what she considered to be *her* bed.

I was barely conscious of Wednesday rolling into
Thursday, but when I woke up on Friday morning, I
felt a million times better. I checked the date on my
bedside clock and sat bolt upright in my bed. I'd lost
two whole days that I could have spent investigating
Matt Malone's missing diamond necklace, not to
mention my shifts at the Movie Theater Café. For all I

knew, Sergeant O'Shea had charged Jennifer Pearce with the crime. I swung my legs over the side of the bed and groped on the nightstand for my phone. I hit Jennifer's number.

"Hullo?" She sounded sleepy, and I checked the clock again. Five o'clock in the morning. *Oops.*

"It's Maggie Doyle. Sorry if I woke you."

"It's okay. I need to get up soon anyway." I heard a door close and assumed she'd moved her location to take this call.

"I'm sorry I haven't started looking into the necklace business. I've been sick."

"Noreen told me," Jennifer said between yawns. "Don't worry about it. Nothing new has happened since you spoke to Aaron on Tuesday. Sergeant O'Shea is still determined to pin the blame on me, but he hasn't charged me yet. Mainly, I suspect, due to the influence of Sergeant Reynolds."

"The sooner Reynolds takes over as the official head of police on Whisper Island, the better," I said. "He, at least, has a functioning brain."

This made Jennifer laugh. "Sergeant O'Shea reminds me of PC Goon in Enid Blyton's *The Five Find-Outers* series."

"I don't think I read that series," I said, casting my mind back over the books I'd borrowed from Julie during childhood summers spent on the island. "Wait a sec...the fool of a policeman who's always outwitted by the gang of kid investigators?"

"That's the one."

"Okay, what do you need me to do?" I asked, turning the conversation back to the investigation. "After losing two days to the flu, I'm not sure where to start. Are Malone's sons still staying at the hotel?"

"Yes, but they seem to spend more time on the golf course and at the golf club bar than at the hotel." Jennifer's voice held a hint of acid. "For two men who claim I've stolen a considerable portion of their inheritance, they appear to be remarkably calm."

"Right." I rooted through my closet for clean clothes. "I'll jump under the shower and head for the golf course."

"It's five in the morning, Maggie," Jennifer said dryly. "Even the most dedicated golfers won't be out before dawn."

"Yeah, that's true." I took a cautious sniff under my arms and recoiled. Two days without washing didn't make for a pretty smell. "Either way, I'm hitting the shower."

Jennifer yawned again. "And I'm hitting the bed until my alarm goes off."

"I'll call you later."

"Thanks, Maggie." Jennifer's voice softened. "I appreciate you doing this for Aaron and me."

"No problem. I owe you one, after all."

I put the phone back on my nightstand and had a luxuriously long shower, after which I, too, collapsed back into my bed for another two hours. When I emerged from my room for the second time that morning, Noreen had left a basket of fresh scones waiting for me on the kitchen table and a note saying she'd hitched a ride into town with Paddy Driscoll and left me the car in case I was feeling better and wanted to get out of the house. I sent her a text message to say thanks, and then added a question about her golf club membership. Her response was swift.

I'll give them a call and tell them to let you in as my guest. I've been a member long enough that they owe me that much. Take it easy, love. You're supposed to be recuperating, not playing golf!

Me playing golf? I laughed at the idea. The only reason I knew one end of a golf club from the other was from a murder investigation I'd worked on back home.

Uncomfortable in the knowledge that I was yet again depriving my aunt of her car, I drove in the direction of the Whisper Island Golf Club. If I wrapped up my oh-so-subtle questioning of the Malone brothers quickly, I'd head to the café and let Noreen take the rest of the day off.

The lady at the Whisper Island Golf Club's reception greeted me with a warm smile. "Come on in, Maggie. Noreen told us to expect you."

The chatty woman was easy to coax into indiscretions about the golf club's guests, and only too happy to inform me that Enda and Mick Malone were having a late breakfast in the club's restaurant. I took this as my cue to express my desire for food and followed the receptionist into the elegantly appointed restaurant.

And ran slap bang into Lenny Logan, my old friend, and Movie Club buddy. We stared at one another, open-mouthed. "What are you doing here?" we demanded in unison.

"Ladies first," Lenny said. "You're not exactly the golf club type."

"Neither are you." I lowered my voice. "I'm trying to accidentally on purpose bump into Matt Malone's sons."

"And I'm here about the chickens," Lenny added as if this information was self-explanatory.

"Chickens?" I gaped at him in bewilderment.

The receptionist cleared her throat, reminding me of her existence, and motioned to a free table. "Will your friend be joining you, Maggie?"

"Yes, he will." I grabbed Lenny's arm and dragged him to the free table. "You can explain about the chickens over breakfast."

"I've already eaten," he protested when the receptionist had gone.

"So have I. We can order a slice of toast and share it. I need to brainstorm something, and you're the perfect person to do it with." I grinned at my friend. "Besides, I need to know about the chickens."

To the waitress's disgust, Lenny and I ordered toast. I added freshly squeezed orange juice and a pot of coffee to our order, which mollified her somewhat.

"So," I said the instant she was out of earshot. "What's all this about chickens?"

"Granddad keeps chickens. Every year, the golf club borrows them for Chicken Night."

Okay, then. Yet another crazy island tradition that I knew nothing about. "You said 'borrow,' so I'm assuming Chicken Night doesn't involve chicken fricassee?"

"Oh, no." Lenny's face was a picture of horror. "We don't *eat* the chickens. We dress them up in little green costumes, and they perform a dance."

I checked my friend for signs he was pranking me, but his bony face wore a serious expression. "Why on earth would anyone want to watch chickens dance? And why would the chickens cooperate?"

"Drunk golfers are weird," Lenny said pragmatically, "but they pay well for the chickens, and Granddad's been their official supplier for years. As for the chickens' motivation—" he shrugged, "—as long as they're fed, they're happy."

Our order arrived, and we fell silent while our waitress placed a rack of crisp toast and an array of jams on the table. After she'd left, Lenny leaned forward. "So why are you looking for the Malone brothers? I heard you were in bed with the flu."

"I was, but I'm feeling better." I cast a look around the room, but I couldn't identify Matt Malone's sons from the restaurant's patrons. There was one table occupied by two men, but they looked like father and son. "Do you recognize the Malone brothers from this crowd?"

"Sure. Second table by the window."

I took another look and my eyes widened. Five men sat at the table Lenny had identified. Two looked to be the right age to be Matt Malone's sons, and the other three were much younger but bore a resemblance to the older men. "Wait a sec...are those Malone's *grandsons*?"

"Yeah. The two with tans are Aussies, and Brendan Malone lives in Galway, like his dad."

I processed this information. "So Crocodile Dundee is the Australian son, Enda, and the Hemsworth brothers lookalikes are his sons."

Lenny snorted with laughter. "Yeah. The lads are Rob and Darren if I remember right. They're a few years younger than us."

"Then the other guy in his fifties must be Mick Malone," I continued, "and the grumpy-looking dude next to him is his son."

"Correct. Mick Malone imports electronic equipment and sells it wholesale. He's one of my parents' suppliers." Lenny's family ran Whisper Island's only electronics store, and my friend worked there in addition to fixing computers on the side. "Mick's son, Brendan, is a pro golfer."

"Hence their obsession with the golf course."

"Exactly." Lenny fixed me with a curious look. "Why are you so interested in the Malones? Does it have something to do with that necklace Jennifer Pearce is accused of stealing?"

"Yes, but keep it to yourself. Aaron and Jennifer have asked me to do a bit of digging."

"Awesome." Lenny's face lit up. "Can I help?"

"I'd appreciate your assistance, but I'm not sure how you can help."

My friend's grin widened. "But I am. You need a way to bump into the Malones and they hardly ever leave the golf club."

"Yeah..." I said, wary of what harebrained scheme was cooking in Lenny's mind.

"And I just so happen to be a member of the golf club, and I'll need an assistant for Chicken Night."

I eyed him with suspicion. "You need an assistant to dress up chickens in little green costumes?"

"Heck, no. It's an excuse for you to tag along."

I shook my head. "I can't believe *you're* a member of the golf club."

"It's not like I actually *play*," he said, horrified that anyone should accuse him of being a golfer. "At least, not when I can help it. Mum's on the board of directors, and she insisted I learn the basics. A dreadfully dull game, but she loves it."

"How do I find out more about Matt Malone's grandsons?"

"Persuade one of them to attend Chicken Night as your date," Lenny said as though this solution were self-evident.

"How? I'll be helping you. Besides, they're all younger than me—"

"Only by a couple of years. You're twenty-nine, right?"

"Yeah." I'd turn thirty in September, but I was blocking that impending milestone from my mind.

"Rob Malone's around twenty-six or twenty-seven. Perfect for you."

I glanced back at the two beefy Australians, and one caught my eye. Heat stained my cheeks, and I cursed my lack of poise around the opposite sex. I forced a smile, hoping the minimal makeup I'd applied before leaving Noreen's house hid the worst of my post-flu pallor.

"What did I tell you?" Lenny said with a laugh. "Rob likes you. All you need to do is persuade him to hang around for a drink after you've helped me and the chickens do our stuff."

I jerked back and turned to Lenny. "How do I go from a sort-of-sultry look across a restaurant to landing a date with the dude?"

"Leave that part to me. First, we need to introduce you." He pushed his chair back and stood. "Come on. I'll do the intros."

he Malones looked up when Lenny and I approached their table. Mick Malone, the brother from Galway, stood and shook Lenny's hand. "I haven't seen you in a while. How are you keeping?"

"Ah, I'm grand," Lenny said in his habitual easy manner. "And yourself?"

"Some old, same old, you know? It's nice to have a golfing break with the lads." Mick gestured to the other men. "You know Brendan, but have you met my brother and nephews?"

A round of introductions and hearty male handshakes followed. I shifted my weight from one foot to the other, hyper aware of the testosterone dominating the proceedings. Lenny turned to me and winked. "This is Maggie, Dermot Doyle's daughter."

Mick Malone's smile was genuine, but his brother,

Enda, focused on my chest. I took an instant dislike to the man.

"I was at school with your father," Mick said. "How's he doing? Still rising in the ranks of the San Francisco Police Department?"

"Yes," I said, and silently added, *but not as high as Mom.*

"Are you two here for a round of golf?" Mick asked.

"Yes," Lenny said at the same time I said, "No."

My friend shot me a warning look.

"We're considering it," I amended.

"Well, you're welcome to join us for a drink at the bar this evening." Mick grinned. "Lenny and I promise not to talk business."

"Ordering supplies is more Mum's department in any case." Lenny looked at me and smiled. "Unfortunately, we're already committed to the Movie Club meeting this evening, but you're welcome to come as our guests."

"Movie Club?" Brendan snorted. "Is that the one run by the old bat who owns the café?"

My chest swelled with indignation. "Watch it, pal. The 'old bat' happens to be my aunt."

Brendan's sneer did nothing to enhance his homely appearance. "So?"

"So don't insult my aunt." I glared at the arrogant young man with ill-disguised antipathy. The guy might be a pro golfer, but his athletic prowess appeared to be his one redeeming feature.

Mick cleared his throat. "Well, uh, it was nice to meet you, Maggie—"

"I'd like to come to the Movie Club meeting," Rob Malone cut in. "When do I need to be there?"

I exhaled in satisfaction. This was the in I'd been hoping for. "We start serving cocktails at eight, and the movie is due to begin at nine."

Rob nodded. "Sounds good. What are you watching?"

"*To Catch a Thief.*"

"Ah, Hitchcock." The man smiled. "I like his stuff."

I shifted my gaze to Rob's brother. "Would you like to join us?"

"Sure. Why not? It's got to be better than listening to Mick and Dad go on and on about Brendan's golfing stats." He rolled his eyes in an exaggerated manner that took some—but not all—of the sting out of his words. "I'm more into Rugby myself."

Lenny looked pointedly at his watch. "I'd better make tracks. I have to talk to Cormac about the chickens."

"Is this for the infamous Chicken Night we keep hearing about?" Rob asked.

"Yeah. My granddad supplies the chickens each year, and Maggie's going to be my assistant."

This was news to me, but I rolled with it. By

helping Lenny with the chickens, I'd have a chance to talk with whichever Malones didn't make it to tonight's Movie Club meeting. Not a bad plan actually.

Lenny and I parted company with the Malones and paid for our barely touched breakfast. Back in the lobby, I asked, "When is this Chicken Night happening?"

"Tomorrow."

I bit my lip. "Noreen wants me to go to the Valentine's dance at the town hall."

"You can do both. The chickens don't appear on stage until ten."

"Darn. I was hoping for an excuse to bail on the dance."

Lenny laughed. "No chance. Your aunts will make sure you and Julie go."

The clock in the lobby chimed the hour. Eleven o'clock. "I'd better get to the café and help Noreen with the lunchtime rush."

"No prob." Lenny slung his backpack over one shoulder. "I need to nail down the details for tomorrow with Cormac Tate. Want me to help set up for the Movie Club meeting later?"

"Yeah, that would be great. Say around seven-thirty?"

"Okay. See you then."

Lenny ambled off to discuss chickens, and I headed back out to the car, my head full of thoughts of missing diamond necklaces. With the revelation that three of Matt Malone's grandsons were on the island, my pool of suspects had widened. My next move was to call Aaron and find out if Malone had left provisions for his grandchildren, and then it was time to negotiate an information exchange with Sergeant Reynolds.

Noreen was grateful to see me show up at the café in time for the lunchtime rush, and I was kept busy for the rest of the day, leaving me no time to call Aaron or Jennifer. I compromised by shooting Jennifer a quick text message, and her response was rapid.

No provisions for his grandchildren. Matt Malone split his wealth four ways between his children. In addition to the necklaces, they'll each receive an equal share of the proceeds of the sale of the Malone farm.

In other words, Matt Malone's grandsons might have a motive for wanting to steal one of the necklaces. While the children would want to make sure they were able to sell the necklaces for their true market value, a grandson strapped for cash wouldn't care if he received less on the black market. But which one? I needed to find out how long the Malones had been on Whisper Island, and if any of them had a police record. And the only way to do the latter was through Sergeant Reynolds.

At seven o'clock, the café closed for the evening, and Noreen and I changed our clothes and began to set up for the Movie Club meeting. "You should have gone home after lunch," I said, handing her a tray of freshly prepared sandwiches to arrange on serving plates. "I could have managed on my own."

"I know, but I didn't want to leave you. You're still not one-hundred percent."

"True, but I'm a lot better than yesterday." I lined up cocktail glasses and checked that I had all the ingredients on hand to make tonight's cocktail menu options. In honor of *To Catch a Thief*'s French Riviera setting, I'd chosen five cocktails to fit the theme: the Rose, the 1789, the Sidecar, the French Martini, and the French Connection.

As promised, Lenny showed up at seven-thirty and set up the projector and other tech equipment that would enable us to show the movie in the small movie theater at the back of the café. When he'd finished taking care of the equipment, Lenny joined me behind the counter. "Well, well. Look who's the first to arrive? Looks like you have an admirer, Maggie."

Rob and Darren Malone entered the café and made a beeline for the counter. I smoothed down my blue evening gown, grateful I'd made an extra effort for tonight's meeting. Much to Noreen's amusement, I'd even attempted to tame my wild red curls for the occasion, but soon gave it up as a lost cause and resorted to my usual messy up-do.

Rob gave me an appreciative once-over. "Hey, Maggie. Looking good."

"Thanks. So are you." And he was. His dark hair was slicked back, and his suit was obviously tailor made. Either Rob Malone had money to burn, or he had expensive tastes. His brother was slightly less formally attired and hadn't bothered with a tie.

Darren glanced at his watch, clearly not happy to be here. "Do you have beer or just this girly stuff?"

"We only serve cocktails at club meetings," I said, keeping my tone breezy, "but I can offer you coffee or a mineral water."

Darren wrinkled his nose in displeasure and pointed to the cocktail menu. "If this stuff is all you've got, I'll try a French Martini."

"Sorry about my brother," Rob said after Darren wandered off to look at the framed vintage movie posters that decorated the walls of the café. "He doesn't get out much in polite society."

I laughed. "Don't worry about it. What would you like to drink?"

"I'm driving, so I'll stick with that mineral water you mentioned."

I poured him a glass of Ballygowan and shoved it across the counter. The café was starting to fill up with club members, and Lenny took care of most of the orders, leaving me free to chat to Rob.

"I was sorry to hear about your grandfather."

"Yeah. He was a nice old geezer." He caught my

look of surprise and laughed. "I didn't know him all that well. We'd only met twice, and the last time was when I was fourteen. He and my dad weren't that close."

"Right. What does your father do in Australia?"

"He runs an import and export business for electronics. Similar to what Mick does over here, but my dad's business is on a larger scale, shall we say." The smug smile dented his laid-back attitude. Either Rob liked the fact that his father was the more successful brother, or he was sick of Mick's boasting about Brendan's golf career and wanted to stick up for the Australian branch of the family.

I refilled his glass and fixed a Sidecar for another club member. Rob made no attempt to mingle, seemingly content to lean against the counter and chat with me. The conversation drifted to Rugby, a topic in which I had no great interest, but I let him prattle on while I shook cocktails and sliced fruit to decorate the glasses. By the time Julie arrived, I was heartily sick of my new friend. Rob was good-looking, sure, but he knew it, and his three favorite topics were me, myself, and I.

My cousin reached the counter at the same time as one of the other members, Günter Hauptmann, a weird German dude who lived on a houseboat all year long. "Ladies first," Günter said in his thick German accent.

"I'll have a French Martini," Julie said to me, before turning to Günter. "I was serious about what I said. You can't stay on the boat tomorrow night. There's a storm forecast."

Günter shrugged. "I've experienced island storms before, and my boat was just fine."

"This one is supposed to be big." Julie rolled her eyes in exasperation. "Men. They always think they're invincible."

"A storm's forecast?" I asked. "I didn't know."

"Well, yeah," my cousin said, looking at me as though I were crazy. "It's been the island's main topic of conversation since yesterday. How did you miss hearing about it?"

"I was sick in bed. I guess I didn't get the memo."

"Oh, that's right. Mum mentioned you'd taken to your bed." A sympathetic look crossed over my cousin's face. "How are you feeling now?"

"Much better, thanks." I held up my glass of mineral water. "But I'm sticking to tea and water for the next couple of days."

Julie nodded. "Smart."

Darren Malone lumbered over to his brother and gave my cousin an unsubtle once-over that brought a flush to her freckled cheeks. "Hey, gorgeous." He stuck out his hand in greeting. "I'm Darren Malone."

Before my cousin could respond, a jangle above the door indicated the arrival of more people. I looked up and swallowed hard. Jennifer Pearce swept in, her head held high, and her fiancé at her side.

"She's got a nerve," Darren Malone growled. "That woman stole my dad's inheritance."

a stunned silence descended over the café. Two red spots appeared on Jennifer Pearce's cheeks, but she made no attempt to engage with Darren Malone.

"Pretty ironic *her* showing up to watch *To Catch a Thief*," Darren continued with a nasty laugh.

"Shut up, you fool," Rob muttered to his brother. "We've got no proof that she stole the necklace."

Darren rounded on him. "Who else could have taken it?"

"You, for one."

We all jerked our heads around to stare at the newcomer. Sergeant Liam Reynolds stood in the doorway, flanked by a reserve policeman on one side and a purple-faced O'Shea on the other.

"I find it interesting that neither your uncle nor your father mentioned their sons were on the island."

Reynolds stepped inside the café. "Care to explain why?"

Darren shot Rob a panicked look, and his brother took the hint. "Why would they tell you we were here?" Rob asked. "It's not like we're inheriting anything from our grandfather's estate. We only care about the stolen necklace because it affects our fathers and aunts."

"Let's discuss this at the station," Reynolds said. "There are a few questions I'd like to ask you."

"Surely this isn't necessary," Sergeant O'Shea broke in, his complexion growing redder by the second. "I've known Mick Malone for years. His nephews wouldn't steal."

"Is that so?" Reynolds fixed Darren with a hard stare, and the young man flushed.

Interesting. My pulse raced. I yearned to get hold of whatever dirt Reynolds had dug up on Darren Malone.

"We'll come to the station," Rob said hastily. "No need to make a fuss."

"There's every need," O'Shea shouted. "This is outrageous. The Malones have been members of the Whisper Island Golf Club for years."

"I suppose," I said in a saccharine tone, "that club members confine themselves to murder, not theft."

This remark elicited a titter of laughter from the club members. O'Shea did not share their amusement. His piggy eyes bulged and his hammy fists clenched.

"Keep out of police business, Ms. Doyle. We don't like meddlers around here."

"This meddler solved a murder last week," Reynolds said softly. "One committed by a member of this club *and* the golf club. Or have you forgotten?"

O'Shea's fleshy lips opened and closed. "Of course not. I just—"

"I don't care who's a member of the Whisper Island Golf Club, and I don't care if your cronies are offended. We're here to do a job, so let's do it."

With obvious reluctance, Sergeant O'Shea accompanied Reynolds, the reserve, and the Malone boys out to the waiting squad car. After they'd driven off, the Movie Club gathering buzzed with gossip about the stolen necklace. I was relieved to see that no one appeared to take the accusations against Jennifer seriously. On the contrary: she was the night's star attraction.

After graciously battling her way through the crowd and fending off a barrage of questions, a flustered Jennifer reached the bar. I slid her a freshly made French Martini. "You look like you could do with refreshment."

"Thanks, Maggie." Jennifer inclined her head in the direction of the door. "Well, that was dramatic. I wonder what Reynolds has found about Darren Malone."

"It's got to be something to do with a robbery," I said, reading between the lines.

"Yeah. That was the impression I got." Jennifer raised her glass to her lips and took a sip of her cocktail. "I had no idea who he was when he started attacking me."

I frowned. "Wait...are you saying you'd never met Darren Malone before tonight?"

"Yeah. I had no idea he was on Whisper Island until you told me about it. My work only concerns Matt Malone's heirs."

"Then how did Darren know who *you* were?"

Jennifer paused in the action of lifting her glass for a second sip. "I don't know. Someone at the club meeting must have told him."

I shook my head. "That's not possible. He identified you the instant you walked through the door. Is your photo on the Nesbitt & Son website?"

"No. On my request, we opted not to use photographs. I value my privacy. And in our case, there's no need. We get our clients through word of mouth on the island."

"Darren must have seen you somewhere and had you pointed out to him." I frowned, a dark suspicion forming in the back of my mind.

"That must be it," Jennifer said, "but I don't see why it's relevant."

"It would be very relevant if he happened to see you with those necklaces. Who knew you were taking them to the mainland to be appraised?"

"Just Aaron and me." Her eyes widened. "I didn't

54

even tell Nick. He'd have blown a gasket if he'd known I was tasked with carrying two-million-euros worth of jewelry to Galway and back."

"Weren't you worried about transporting the necklaces?"

She blinked. "Well, yes, but it was my job."

A job that Jennifer took seriously. Too seriously, some might argue, which made me even less inclined to believe her capable of stealing from her clients. My eyes strayed to the door of the café. I seriously needed to learn more about Darren Malone, and I intended to do it tonight.

*a*t eleven o'clock on Friday night, I peered over the bushes of Mamie Byrne's garden. "Still no sign of Reynolds."

"Are you sure a stakeout's necessary?" Lenny asked between mouthfuls of fish and chips. "And wouldn't we be more likely to find the sarge at the station rather than Mamie's B&B?"

"This is more likely to be a Sergeant O'Shea-free zone," I pointed out. "How can I interrogate Reynolds about the case if O'Shea's skulking in the background?"

"Speaking of skulking," said a familiar deep voice behind us, "what are you two doing spying on Mamie's place?"

I whirled around to face a bemused Sergeant Reynolds. Arms folded across his broad chest, his fair hair appeared blonder under the glare of the streetlight.

Aware of his scrutiny, I felt my cheeks grow warm. "We were waiting for you."

Reynolds's mouth twitched. "Since when does waiting for me involve scaring my landlady into thinking you were burglars casing the joint?"

"Oops," I said. "Sorry about that."

"I told you I saw a curtain twitch," Lenny said, stuffing another chip into his mouth.

"You'd better come in before Mamie decides I'm in imminent danger of being murdered." Reynolds opened the gate and gestured for us to walk up the path.

Sure enough, the proprietor of Apple Tree Lodge Bed and Breakfast was hovering just inside the door, armed with a rolling pin. She slow-blinked when she saw Lenny and me. "Oh, it's you two. I thought the place was about to be ransacked."

"Sorry about that, Mamie," I said, shame-faced. "We didn't want to wake up you or your guests so late."

The older woman lowered her rolling pin. "Sure, I have no guests this time of year, excepting the sergeant."

"And I'm very grateful you were willing to take me in until my cottage is ready," Sergeant Reynolds said dutifully. "Sorry about the late night visitors. They're helping me on a case."

Slightly mollified, Mamie's lined face relaxed, and she brushed invisible lint off the polyester pantsuit that had been fashionable circa 1976. She eyed Lenny and me with a dubious expression. "I suppose you'll be wanting tea." Her gaze dropped to the fish-and-chip container in Lenny's hand. "And a plate for those."

My friend beamed at her. "Thanks, Mamie."

When his landlady bustled off to the kitchen, Reynolds ushered Lenny and me into the bed and breakfast's communal living room. "You'd better keep your voices low," he warned.

"Yeah," Lenny said loudly. "Mamie listens at doors."

I exchanged a look with Reynolds and rolled my eyes. "Okay. As you've probably guessed, we're here to get the dirt on Darren Malone."

Reynolds regarded me with a bland expression that was belied by the amused twinkle in his eyes. "What makes you think I'll discuss an active case with you?"

"Because Lenny and I can help," I said boldly. Okay, I wasn't sure how, but I'd wing the conversation and see if I hit upon a good idea.

"Want a chip?" Lenny extended his fish-and-chip container to Reynolds.

"No, thanks. I'm more interested in knowing how you and Maggie think you can assist me."

"Chicken Night," Lenny said, deadpan. "We can spy on the Malones."

Sergeant Reynolds' jaw descended. Before he could ask for clarification, Mamie bustled in with a tea tray and a plate and cutlery for Lenny's takeout meal. "I never liked the Malone boys," she said, placing cups and saucers before each of us. "They were always trouble."

"I assume you're referring to Enda and Mick," I said. "Or did you mean their sons?"

"I don't know their sons. I hear mention of the golfing lad from time to time, but I couldn't put a face to a name. No, I meant Enda and Mick." Mamie looked at each of us in turn. "We were at school together, you know."

I choked on my tea and performed a mental readjustment of Mamie's age.

"It's the clothes," Lenny said under his breath, and I bit my tongue to stop myself from laughing.

"Why didn't you like Mick and Enda Malone?" Reynolds asked. "And what sort of trouble were you referring to?"

Mamie sniffed. "They were wild as children, and bullies in school. There were rumors about Mick getting a girl pregnant, but I never found out if that was true. As for Enda..." Her voice trailed off on an ominous note. "He had a tendency to take things that didn't belong to him."

"He was a thief?" I glanced at Reynolds and then turned back to Mamie. "What did he steal?"

The older woman pursed her lips. "Nothing was ever proven, mind, but the word was that Enda was behind a raid on the post office. The thieves made off with over five hundred pounds, and the poor postmaster suffered a bad concussion."

"Pounds?" It took a moment for the penny to drop. "Oh, right. You used to have pounds in Ireland before euros were introduced."

"Pounds or euros, it was a lot of money at the time, especially from a small post office. And assaulting a postmaster..." Mamie clucked her tongue. "A disgrace, that's what it was. No one was sorry to see Enda go to Australia."

"Enda Malone has no criminal record," Reynolds said. "Do you know if he was questioned at the time of the assault and robbery?"

Mamie nodded, and her plump cheeks quivered with indignation. "Without proof, the police had to let him go."

"Thanks for the tea and info, Mamie," Reynolds said, deftly bringing the conversation to a close. "There's no need for you to stay up. I'll lock up when Maggie and Lenny leave."

His landlady regarded Lenny and me with disapproval. "Okay, but don't forget to switch on the dishwasher before you go to bed."

"No worries. I'll take care of it."

With obvious reluctance, Mamie removed herself from our presence. The instant the door closed behind his landlady, I pounced. "What did you discover about Darren Malone?"

Reynolds laughed. "No way. You and Lenny have yet to convince me that you can help me with the case. I'm not sharing any info with you unless there's a reason." He paused. "But I've got to know what Chicken Night is."

Lenny provided him with a brief rundown of the Whisper Island Golf Club and its tradition of dancing chickens. "So," Lenny concluded, "Maggie and I will have the perfect opportunity to observe the Malones. And with Rob Malone having the hots for Maggie, we can pump them for info. After a couple of shots of my grandfather's poteen, they'll tell us everything we want to know."

I didn't share my friend's confidence in our persuasive abilities, but having the chance to party with the Malones was an opportunity the police wouldn't have. "We can chat to them in an informal context," I said. "That's not something you can do, particularly now that you've questioned Rob and Darren."

Reynolds stared at me for a long moment. "Sergeant O'Shea is a member of the golf club. I'll bet he'll be at Chicken Night."

"Who's going to confide in that eejit?" Lenny demanded.

"So says the man who's just confessed that he'll be herding a troop of dancing chickens and wearing a leprechaun outfit for the occasion," Reynolds said mildly, and I struggled not to laugh.

"I can assure you that I won't be dressed as a leprechaun," I said. "I'll chat up the Malone boys and see if I can persuade them to let something slip."

Reynolds sighed. "Okay. I want this necklace business cleared up, and I don't think Jennifer or Aaron had anything to do with its disappearance, but I need your word that this information will stay between us."

"Scout's honor," Lenny said, his face the picture of innocence.

"I promise," I added, doubting my friend had ever been a boy scout, but not willing to argue the point when Reynolds was on the verge of telling me what I wanted to know.

Reynolds leaned back in his chair. "Darren Malone was a suspect in a bank robbery in Sydney two years ago. Like the post office robbery that Mamie described, the police couldn't make the charges stick, and they had to let him go. However, the officer in charge of the case is convinced Darren did it and has been keeping tabs on him ever since."

I whistled. "An experienced bank robber could probably get his paws on a necklace in an unguarded safe. The security system at Jennifer and Aaron's place leaves a lot to be desired."

"I want you and Lenny to glean whatever information you can from the Malones, and report back to me. Specifically, I want to know if they knew Jennifer by sight before Darren's outburst at the Movie Club meeting. And I also need to find out what, exactly, Rob and Darren's financial situation is. I'm assuming the golfer, Brendan, is doing okay, but if you can check on him, too, all the better."

Lenny and I stood to leave. "You've got it, Sarge," I said. "We'll do our best and report back to you on Sunday. Should we meet you here?"

Reynolds escorted us back into the hallway and opened the front door. "Yeah. Here would be good. Say ten o'clock in the morning?"

"We'll be here. Right, Lenny?"

Lenny nodded enthusiastically. "Sure thing."

"Good night," Reynolds said with a smile. "And good luck with the chickens—human and fowl."

As we walked toward the gate, Lenny turned to me. "Um...Maggie? About my leprechaun costume..."

My heart sank. "No way. Absolutely not."

My friend grinned. "You know you're expected to wear one, too, right?"

8

*W*hen Saturday evening rolled around, my prayers for a relapse of the flu hadn't been answered. The Valentine's Day dance loomed, followed by Lenny's infamous Chicken Night. With an air of gloomy resignation, I regarded the two outfits spread across Julie's bed.

"The leprechaun dress has a certain charm," my cousin said. "If it were St. Patrick's Day. And if I were drunk."

I groaned. "I can't believe I agreed to this."

"Are you referring to the dancing chickens, or to a spin around the dance floor with Paddy Driscoll?" Julie's eyes twinkled with merriment.

"Both." I fingered the green felt of my leprechaun costume. "Although my dress for the Valentine's dance is preferable to this outfit. I can't believe your mother found me a leprechaun costume."

"Before she started working at the library full-time, Mum was a leading light in the Whisper Island Dramatic Society. She still has connections, and they were only too happy to provide her with a female leprechaun costume."

"It's like a cross between every preschooler's nightmare, and a stripper's outfit."

"You'll be fine," Julie said, her sincerity undermined by her struggle not to laugh. "Lenny will be wearing a similar outfit."

"So we'll both look like dorks. That image doesn't bring me comfort."

"Maybe the dance with Paddy will cheer you up. Speaking of dancing..." my cousin glanced at her watch, "...we'd better get moving if we're to make it to the town hall on time."

I grabbed the blue dress I was wearing for the first part of my evening. "Give me five, and I'll be ready."

I was as good as my word, even if I was still attempting to tame my mane when Julie pulled her MINI into the town hall's parking lot fifteen minutes later.

She eyed my efforts with the brush. "From one curly-haired woman to another, give up, and let me have a go," Julie said.

I handed over the brush, along with the fancy clip I'd somehow thought I could wrestle into my hair. "I always think I can make it look good," I said, as my cousin ruthlessly attacked my scalp. "But I never can."

Julie pulled my stubborn curls into an updo and secured it in place with the clip. "There," she said, pleased with her handiwork. "That's about as good as it'll get. Ready to go inside?"

"No." I opened the passenger door. "But I'll never hear the end of it if I don't."

I climbed out of the car and narrowly avoided stepping into a deep puddle. The heavy February rain had formed a series of glistening puddles in the parking lot, and raindrops pounded against my waterproof coat. Julie and I extended our umbrellas and ran for the entrance.

Inside the town hall, the dance was in full swing. Several of Whisper Island's older couples were on the dance floor, performing performed steps I vaguely recognized from old movies, but could never recreate.

"Finally." Noreen grabbed our arms and hauled us over to a refreshment stand where Julie's parents were helping themselves to drinks.

Uncle John wore a pained expression on his craggy face. "Every year, it's the same story. Bad music, worse food, and watered-down whiskey."

"Ah, would you ever stop with your whiskey accusations," Philomena said. "It's all in your head. No one's diluting the drinks."

John grunted and gave Julie and me a conspiratorial wink. "What can I get you lovely young ladies?"

"How about a one-way ticket out of here?" I cast a

jaundiced gaze around the crowd. "Is it my imagination or are Julie and I the only people here who are under fifty?"

"Who are you calling fifty?" yelled Sadie Levin as her husband swung her past on the dance floor. "Sure I'm only forty-nine."

"You've been forty-nine for the last five years, Sadie," Noreen yelled back. "Time to bring out the correct number of candles."

John lifted a bottle of lemonade and examined its label. "Sure, this is the cheap stuff."

His wife rolled her eyes. "Stop bellyaching about the drinks and serve the girls."

John looked at Julie and me. "We've got water, lemonade, diluted whiskey, and some awful white wine that's sweet enough to make your teeth fall out."

"An enticing array of beverages," I said dryly. "I'll have a glass of lemonade."

"I'll stick to water tonight, Dad," Julie added. "I need to drive Maggie to Chicken Night at nine-thirty."

My uncle's brow creased in concern. "Be careful, love. There's a storm forecast."

Julie rolled her eyes. "Yes, Dad. I'll take shelter if it gets bad."

My uncle poured us our drinks and then raised his whiskey glass to us. "*Slàinte.*"

I'd barely had a chance to take a sip from my glass when the main doors swung open, ushering in a gale-force wind and a disheveled-looking Günter and

67

Reynolds. My hands were clammy around my glass, and my mouth grew dry. After the men had stripped off their raincoats and deposited them with a cloakroom attendant, they made a beeline for us.

"Oh, for heaven's sake," Julie muttered. "Does Günter have to show up everywhere I go?"

"He mightn't be here for you," I teased. "He might have fallen for Noreen's charms."

Under the disco lights, my cousin's cheeks grew pink. "Not that I care, of course."

I swallowed a laugh. Julie cared far more about Günter than she liked to admit. But then, who was I to criticize? The instant I'd clapped eyes on Reynolds, my vow to avoid men until I could trust myself to pick a good one took a flying leap out the window.

As he and Günter maneuvered their way through the crowd, Reynolds's gaze met mine. My breath caught for an instant, and I took a hasty swig from my lemonade glass. If he asked me to dance, would I say yes? What a ridiculous question. I was already imagining his strong arms around my waist. My heart beat faster.

The men had almost reached us when my glass was whipped out of my hand, and I found myself swung onto the dance floor.

"Sorry, Maggie," Paddy Driscoll said with a grimace. "I promised Noreen I'd dance with you. Better get it over with, eh?"

Not exactly the dance partner I'd been hoping for.

"No need to be polite on my account, Paddy. If you'd rather ask someone else to dance—?"

"Ah, no." The taciturn farmer twirled me around, deftly avoiding a collision with an elderly woman's walker. "I don't like this type of shindig, but Noreen says it does me good once a year or so."

I bit the inside of my cheek to stop from laughing. "So this is like your annual attempt to be sociable?"

Paddy grunted. "I show up to the Movie Club, don't I?"

"You do," I conceded, "but you're grumpy, and you only talk to one or two people." I didn't add that those conversations were usually about sheep.

"Evening."

The deep voice tugged my attention away from my dance partner. A bemused Sergeant Reynolds swung past us with Rita Ahearn, the local fire chief's wife, clinging to his chest. An unfamiliar stab of jealousy made me catch my breath for the second time that evening.

"Maggie, watch out," Paddy roared.

Too late. The couple with the walkers danced by us, and the heel of one of my shoes caught against the frame. Before I could register what was happening, I'd pitched forward and landed face first in a guy's lap.

With as much dignity as I could muster under the circumstances, I removed my face from the man's crotch and struggled to my feet, wincing in pain when I placed weight on my right ankle. "Sorry about that."

"No problem," the old man rasped. "Most fun I've had in years."

"Are you all right, Maggie?" Paddy asked, appearing at my side with a concerned expression on his face. "Did you hurt your foot?"

"Put it this way: my ankle had a fight with a walker, and the walker won."

My new friend loved this and patted the empty seat next to his wheelchair. "Come and sit with me for a while."

I glanced at Paddy. "Sorry, but I don't think I'm up to more dancing."

"Okay. Do you want me to get Noreen?"

I shook my head. "No thanks. I'll take the weight off my ankle and it'll be okay."

I sank onto the seat next to the guy in the wheelchair, grateful to take the pressure off my sore ankle. "I don't believe we've met."

"No, but I know who you are," the old man said with a chuckle. "You're Maggie Doyle, Noreen and Philomena's niece."

"That's right, but I don't know your name."

"I'm Rick O'Mara. I was head of police here on Whisper Island before I retired." The old man's eyes twinkled. "I've heard a lot about you."

"Sergeant O'Shea and I aren't exactly on the best of terms."

This was an understatement, and we both knew it.

When Sergeant O'Mara leaned forward in his

chair, his bones creaked. "I hear Aaron Nesbitt has hired you to find that missing necklace."

"Yes," I said warily, "but I can't talk about—"

"Those Malone boys were always trouble," he said as though he hadn't heard me. "I suppose you heard about the raid on the post office?"

"Of course," I breathed. "You must have been the officer in charge when that happened."

The man nodded. "A terrible business. The postmaster was never the same after the robbery."

I frowned. "I heard he suffered a concussion. Was it more serious than that?"

"Not physically, but emotionally. He'd always suffered from his nerves, and the robbery was too much for him."

"I'm sorry to hear that."

The old man eyed me shrewdly. "Which of the Malones do you believe stole that necklace?"

"I haven't decided yet. Enda and Mick might have done it. So might one of their sons." I volleyed the question back to him. "Which of the brothers did you believe was responsible for the post office robbery?"

"Both," he replied without hesitations. "Mick always had a temper, but Enda had the brains. The robbery was too well planned for that to have been Mick's idea. The fact that the postmaster walked in was pure chance. The man was supposed to be in Galway for the day, but stayed home due to a migraine."

A migraine that was unlikely to have been helped by getting whacked over the head. "Poor guy."

"Yeah." The old man's wizened frame appeared to shrink. "I regret that I never managed to solve that case."

An idea, hazy and half-formed, lurked at the back of my mind. "Does the postmaster's family still live on Whisper Island?"

"Only the daughter. The man himself died years ago, and his wife is in a nursing home in Galway."

I sucked in a breath. Could the postmaster's daughter have heard about the necklaces Matt Malone had purchased as his children's inheritance? Had she then decided to steal one as revenge for the attack on her father? "I'd like to talk to the postmaster's daughter," I said. "She might be able to provide me with background info on the Malone brothers."

Sergeant O'Mara snorted. "I should say so. The poor girl had to go to school with those bullies."

A memory pinged in my brain, and my pulse picked up the pace. "What's her name?"

"Mamie Byrne," the retired policeman said. "She runs the Apple Tree Lodge B&B."

9

*E*very cell in my body buzzed with excitement. If the Malone brothers had been responsible for her father's injury, Mamie Byrne had good reason to hate them. Why hadn't she mentioned the attack when we'd discussed the case at her B&B? Was it because she had something to hide?

I looked at the retired police officer. "Thanks for the info, Sergeant O'Mara. I want to do everything I can to find the necklace and clear Jennifer Pearce's name."

A smile lit up his craggy face. "Good girl."

I slipped a receipt out of my purse and scribbled my number on the back. "If you can think of anything else relating to the Malone brothers or the attack on the postmaster, please give me a call."

The old man folded the receipt and put it into his

shirt pocket. "I've told you all I remember, but if something else occurs to me, I'll be in touch."

After I'd left Sergeant O'Mara, I went in search of Reynolds. I found him by the fire exit, chatting to Günter.

"Are you guys planning your escape already?"

They looked up when I spoke, and Reynolds's warm smile melted my composure.

"How's your foot?" he asked, barely containing his amusement. "We saw you fall, and Paddy said you'd twisted your ankle."

"I'd imagine *everyone* witnessed me fall face first into a guy's crotch," I said dryly. "As for my ankle, it feels better than it did when I'd first injured it, but I have a slight limp."

Reynolds laughed. "Does this mean I won't be able to persuade you to dance with me this evening? You were showing such enthusiasm on the dance floor with Paddy."

"Haha," I said sarcastically. "These old dances aren't my thing. I'm not sorry to have an excuse to sit them out."

Although I very much regretted not being able to dance with Reynolds. I'd fantasized about his strong arms guiding me around the dance floor far more than I should have.

I glanced at Günter. "Can I borrow the sarge for a few minutes? There's something I need to discuss with him."

Günter's easy smile widened. "Sure. In the meantime, I'll go and annoy Julie. I'm good at that."

"Play nicely," I warned, but Günter just laughed. After Günter had ambled off in search of my cousin, I turned to Reynolds and shook my head. "Those two are ridiculous."

He held his palms up. "I'm not getting involved. They're more tempestuous than the storm that's forecast. If you're heading out to the Golf Club later, promise me you'll stay there if the storm gets bad."

I made a mock salute. "Yes, Sarge. We'll stay at the Golf Club all night if the weather gets wild."

"Smart. Now, what did you want to talk to me about?"

"I have some info for you regarding the missing necklace case."

Reynolds sighed. "It's not my case, Maggie. All I can do is pass on whatever you've discovered to Sergeant O'Shea."

"Even if it concerns Mamie?"

His eyes widened. "Why would Mamie be mixed up with the missing necklace? Do you suspect she stole it?"

"If she did, it wouldn't necessarily be for monetary gain." I gave Reynolds a brief breakdown of my conversation with Sergeant O'Mara, culminating with Mamie's connection to the postmaster allegedly attacked by the Malones.

Reynolds rubbed his freshly shaven jaw. "I'll talk to

75

Mamie. I've gotten to know her pretty well over the last few weeks. Even if she has a grudge against the Malones, I can't see her standing by and saying nothing while Jennifer Pearce's name is dragged through the mud."

"It doesn't fit with my impression of her, either, but people do surprising things, especially if they've let resentment fester for years."

"True." Reynolds gaze fixed on the crowd behind me. "Julie's waving over at us. I think she wants you to leave."

"Oh, heck." My eyes flew to my watch. "I hadn't realized how late it was. I'll go and say goodbye to my aunts and uncle."

Reynolds caught my arm before I could leave. His grasp was gentle, but the heat from his fingers set my skin tingling. "Be careful, Maggie. If the Malones are capable of attacking an unarmed man, they won't hesitate to hurt you. And a diamond necklace valued at half a million euros is worth a lot more than the five hundred pounds that were taken from the post office."

"I won't take any unnecessary risks," I said, careful to keep my face neutral. If Reynolds thought any inquiry into an object worth that amount was risk-free, he was deluding himself.

"Maggie..." he said in a warning tone as if reading my mind.

On impulse, I blew him a kiss, realizing too late

what I'd done. Heat seared my cheeks. Reynolds blinked but grinned.

"I won't do anything stupid," I said. "And that's all I'm promising."

With these words, I waved and melted into the crowd.

~

It was nearly ten by the time Julie and I arrived at the Whisper Island Golf Club. While Julie headed for the bar, I raced up the steps and tore through the lobby toward the room at the back of the building where Lenny and his chickens were preparing for their performance. I arrived, breathless and disheveled, but with enough time to change my outfit and touch up my makeup.

The changing room was chaotic. Ten chickens strutted around in their green velvet costumes, squawking and divesting themselves of their velvet hats.

"They're an absolute menace," Lenny said, exasperated. "I can't get them to keep their hats on. I don't know how Granddad does it."

"Hang on a minute. Haven't you done this before?"

Lenny looked horrified. "Heck, no. I've helped Granddad out with hauling chickens, but this is my first time choreographing the performance. I only agreed because of his dodgy hip. He's not up to gyrating on stage."

My jaw descended. "Gyrating? We're expected to dance?"

"Well, 'dance' is a bit of an exaggeration." Lenny grimaced. "Sort of leap around the place like a leprechaun."

I choked back a laugh. "Have you ever seen a leprechaun?"

My UFO-fanatic friend gave my question serious consideration before answering. "No," he said regretfully. "But I keep an eye out all the same."

"If you've never seen one, how do you know how leprechauns dance?"

"I haven't a clue, but people expect them to be merry." At my horrified expression, he added. "Sure, it'll be grand. We'll wing it."

One of the chickens marched past me, squawking loudly.

"Poor choice of words," I said in a bone-dry tone.

A knock sounded on the door, and a dapper little man in a tuxedo peeked in. "Are you ready, Lenny? Everyone's waiting."

"Uh, yeah. Give us a sec, Niall. We'll be right out."

"Right-o." Niall nodded at me and closed the door.

Lenny and I looked at each other. "Ready?" he asked.

I cast an eye over his leprechaun costume. He wore green velvet breeches with a matching waistcoat and blazer. His stockings were emblazoned with garish shamrocks and pots of gold. He'd completed the ensemble with a tall black hat decorated with a green sash. He looked absurd.

Lenny grinned. "Go on. Laugh. You know you want to."

"Oh my gosh," I said between heaves. "Laughing is not good for my dress. I think my boobs are going to fall out."

"Try not to breathe," was Lenny's sage advice.

I pulled my shoulders back and took one last look at myself in the mirror. "I look like a St. Patrick's Day stripper."

"You look fab, Maggie," Lenny said. "Now come on. We need to herd the chickens out and let them strut their stuff."

Outside our changing room, Lenny led me down a narrow corridor. He glanced over his shoulder and said, "This leads to the back of the stage."

The chickens waddled along beside us. Judging by their speed, they were excited to be on the move.

Lenny stopped outside a black door and opened it for us. He ushered me in, and the chickens followed. The back of the stage was dark. The chickens seemed to find this alarming. Their squawks increased in intensity, but they allowed Lenny to hoist them onto the stage.

While Lenny got the chickens in order, I climbed the four steps up to the stage and surveyed my surroundings. Beyond the closed curtain, the audience was growing restless. We were a few minutes late, and impatience was mounting.

Lenny wiped sweat from his brow. "Okay. I think we're good to go. Are you ready?"

"Heck, no. Are you?"

He laughed. "Absolutely not."

"Excellent. Let's do this thing." I took a deep breath—or as deep as my tight bodice would allow—and took a step forward. One of the chickens got in my way, forcing me to shift my weight onto my bad ankle.

With my attention focused at floor level, I cast my gaze over the chickens, and my stomach sank. "Um, Lenny? How many chickens did you say there were?"

His hand on the curtain pull froze. "Ten. Why?"

"Then we have a problem. There are only nine here."

10

*L*enny and I stared at one another in horror. "Before we panic, let's do a recount," I said, trying not to laugh and failing miserably.

My friend tugged at his scraggly goatee and groaned. "You're right. There are only nine chickens on stage. It looks like Dooley is missing."

I lost my battle against laughter. "Dooley?" I asked between heaves. "The chickens have names?"

Lenny looked indignant. "Of course they do. These are the Chicken Night dancers. Granddad gives them special treatment."

"In other words, they're not destined to end up in a stew?"

One of the chickens let out a loud squawk. If I hadn't known better, I'd have sworn it was glaring at me.

"You've gone and upset Raggles, Maggie. He's the temperamental one, but a talented dancer."

Lenny's serious tone and expression made me laugh all the louder.

Niall, the guy who'd knocked on our dressing room door earlier, came back stage, a scowl etched across his face. "Are you two ever going to come on stage? The crowd is getting restless."

Lenny cast me a helpless look. "What are we going to do?"

"You'll go on stage with the nine chickens we have, and I'll go in search of the tenth."

Niall's mouth gaped. "You're missing a chicken?" he spluttered. "Where is it?"

I resisted the urge to roll my eyes. "If we knew that, I wouldn't need to look for it."

"We can't have a chicken wandering around the club unsupervised." Niall wiped sweat from his brow and made a vain attempt to loosen his bow tie. "You'll have to find it fast."

"I'm on it." I gave Lenny a thumbs up. "Break a leg. I'll be back with Dooley a.s.a.p."

At that moment, the curtain slid apart, and I darted for the exit.

Niall trundled after me, red-faced and sweating.

"You okay? I don't want to waste time doing CPR if you keel over."

"I'm all right." He tugged at his collar again. "I get stressed organizing events, and I have to supervise the storm preparations. Any idea where your rogue chicken might have gone?"

"No clue. My only experience with chickens is cooking them."

"Fantastic," he muttered. "We'll have bird droppings all over the place."

After a thorough search of the rooms along the corridor at the back of the stage, Niall and I moved toward the golf club's lobby. "We'll start at the entrance and move back," I said. "Dooley has to be around here somewhere."

Outside, the wind was gaining force. The windows of the Whisper Island Golf Club rattled, and a boom of thunder accompanied a flash of lighting.

While we searched for the errant chicken, members of staff scurried around, securing the windows and doors.

"The storm's going to hit in earnest at any moment," Niall said, his round face pinched with worry. "I hope my house will be all right. My cat will be terrified."

"My aunt asked her friends to look after her pets tonight." The Spinsters—regulars at the Movie Theatre Café and good friends of Noreen—had been only too delighted to stay the night at Noreen's cottage. Their house was closer to the sea and likely to be worse hit by the storm.

"I would have sent the cat to my mum," Niall said as he guided me down another corridor of the club, "but she was determined to attend Chicken Night."

I laughed. "I hear it's a huge draw for the islanders."

"I don't recall my mother attending before." Niall looked bemused. "It must be the draw of those Malones. I swear the place is packed because of them."

"Seriously? I didn't get the impression that the Malone brothers were all that popular on Whisper Island. I've yet to find someone who has a good word to say about them."

Niall smirked. "Oh, they aren't popular. I suspect that's the draw. It's like an unofficial school reunion at tonight's Chicken Dance. Plenty of people have old grudges against the Malones and want to see if they've gone to seed since their days of terrorizing their classmates."

"Wow. People I couldn't stand are the reason you couldn't pay me enough to roll up to one of my high school reunions."

"Ah sure, you know how it is on Whisper Island. Not much to do except talk about other people. No one wants to miss out on an opportunity to gather fodder for gossip." The man paused in front of a door and threw it open. "I know chickens can't open doors, but there's a good chance people have been in and out of the billiards room. They don't always remember to close the door behind them."

We searched the empty room from top to bottom, but there was no sign of Dooley.

"What's your role in the club?" I asked after we'd moved on from the billiards room and were searching through a closet in the corridor.

The man beamed. "Officially, I'm the club manager, but in practice, I'm a bit of an odd job man. The club only has a few people on its payroll, as well as the elected positions."

"Sounds like you're kept busy."

"We're a small club, so we all chip in to get stuff done."

I gave the storage closet a final look and stood back. "No luck here."

"That chicken must be somewhere. Do you know when it went missing?"

I shook my head. "I didn't take a head count until Lenny and I were back stage. I'm assuming they were all present and correct before we left the changing room, but I can't be certain."

Niall frowned. "If the chicken did a runner between the changing room and the back stage door, we've covered all the options."

I caught his drift and leaped on the implications. "But if Dooley disappeared back stage, he could have hidden behind equipment or the curtains. It was pretty dark back there."

The man nodded. "Okay. Let's head back to where we started and search behind the stage."

I followed Niall back down the corridor and up the short flight of steps that led to the back of the stage. Beyond the second curtain, the audience roared with laughter at Lenny's antics on stage. From my friend's flustered instructions to the chickens, I got the impression that this year's Chicken Night had turned into an inadvertent comedy routine.

Suddenly, my shoe encountered an unexpected texture beneath it. I looked down and spotted a small green hat. I scooped it up and identified the name Dooley stitched onto the rim. "I have his hat," I told Niall excitedly. "That means he made it as far as back stage with us."

Niall opened his mouth as if to respond when a piercing screech from the audience drew our attention to the stage. A loud squawk followed, producing an even louder human scream.

"Dooley." I dashed to the back curtain and was on the stage with Lenny and his dancing troupe before I'd had time to consider my actions.

The runaway chicken perched on a woman's lap, wings flapping. The cacophony drew squawks of sympathy from the chickens on stage. When Dooley chose this moment to deposit a large quantity of droppings on the woman's dress, the noise rose to a crescendo. Lenny's dancing troupe decided to come to their friend's rescue, and exited the stage at speed, leaving a litany of feathers and green caps in their wake. Between the screaming, squawking, and laughing, Chicken Night was rapidly descending into a farce.

One of the chickens darted between my legs, forcing me to shift my weight onto my bad ankle. Realizing my mistake too late, I yowled in pain and stumbled over a second chicken. Before I had time to react, I'd pitched forward and fallen off the stage.

Before I hit the ground, someone ran forward and broke my fall. We tumbled to the floor in an inelegant heap. The bodice of my costume made a rending sound, and it was suddenly easier to breathe. This could mean only one thing...

"Um, Maggie?" A winded Sergeant Reynolds stared up at me, flushed and uncomfortable. "Your bodice..."

My hands flew to my chest, but all I could do was cover up my exposed cleavage. "What are you doing here?" I demanded of my rescuer. "I thought you intended to spend the evening at the Valentine's Day Dance."

I climbed off him, and we both got to our feet, me still holding my ripped bodice together. Reynolds shrugged out of his uniform jacket and draped it around my shoulders. His lips twitched. "That should preserve your modesty."

"What's left of it," I responded dryly. "Seriously, though, why are you here? Did something happen?"

His expression grew grave, and he turned to address the crowd. "I'm here to get volunteers. The storm's worse than we'd expected, and buildings in Smuggler's Cove are flooding. The mobile phone mast must be damaged because no one has a signal. We need all members of the volunteer fire brigade and paramedics team to help, and anyone else who's willing."

Rob Malone got to his feet. "I'm in the Australian Army, and my brother's in the reserves. We'll go."

The golfer, Brendan Malone, scowled but stood to join his Australian cousins. "I'll help."

Others got to their feet, and Sergeant Reynolds soon had a solid team of volunteers, all of who had received their orders.

"Looks like my first time as the Chicken Dance leader will be my last," Lenny said, removing his ridiculous leprechaun hat. "If you take care of the chickens, I'll go and help combat the flood damage."

"Maybe I can persuade Niall to look after them, and then I can join you." My gaze swept over the audience who'd gathered to watch our disastrous performance and located Niall. He was whispering to an older woman I recognized as Mary Driscoll, the secretary at Aaron and Jennifer's legal practice. I stared harder, and my heart rate kicked up a notch. Could it be...?

Lenny made to move toward Reynolds, but I grabbed his arm. "Does Mary Driscoll have a child?"

My friend looked surprised by my question. "Well, yeah. She's Niall's mum."

I looked back at Niall. He'd said his mother had been at school with the Malone brothers. That put her in her mid-fifties, and Niall had to be ten years older than me, which made him around forty. I cast my mind back to the night in Mamie Byrne's living room. What had Mamie said about rumors surrounding the Malone brothers? Hadn't she mentioned Mick Malone allegedly getting a girl pregnant?

"Lenny," I whispered. "Do you know who Niall's father is?"

He blinked. "No idea. I don't think Mary ever said. She had him young. I know that much. I guess that caused a scandal back in the day."

"Do you remember Mamie Byrne telling us about Mick Malone getting a girl pregnant? What if the girl was Mary, and the baby was Niall?"

Lenny sucked air through his teeth. "Their ages fit."

"Yeah. And it would give both of them a strong motive for wanting to steal Mick Malone's inheritance."

"And Mary works for Aaron and Jennifer—" Lenny said.

"—And could have discovered the code to the safe," I continued, "despite what her employers believe."

The volunteers began to leave the room and head to their cars.

"We need to tell Sergeant Reynolds. If both Mamie and the Driscolls have a motive for doing the Malones harm, the police need to stop focusing on Jennifer as the culprit."

"I agree, but now's probably not the moment. Come on. Let's get changed and go to Smuggler's Cove. There's got to be some way we can help."

By the time Lenny and I had changed back into our street clothes, and I'd persuaded a very reluctant Niall to take charge of the chickens, the rest of the volunteers had all left. We made a beeline for the lobby when the front door of the club burst open. A panic-stricken Noreen stood on the threshold, her hair in disarray. When she saw us, relief flooded her face. "Come quickly. We need your help."

I rushed forward. "What's happened?"

"It's Günter. He got word that his houseboat was adrift and he went out to try to save it. The storm's so wild it began to sink. Some fishermen are helping, but..." she trailed off on a choke.

"Where's Günter?" I demanded, already fearing the worst.

My aunt's terrified eyes met mine. "Still on the boat."

11

*T*he floor seemed to shift beneath my feet. If Günter were aboard a sinking boat in this storm, he'd have no choice but to swim to the shore. I sucked in a breath. I'd seen the size of the waves around Whisper Island on days with a mild wind. The idea of those waves in a storm sent a shiver of fear down my spine. "How many people are trying to help Günter?"

"Three fishermen tried to sail out to him, but the waves forced them back." Noreen's lips trembled. "Günter's an able seaman, but I've seen too many people drown in the bay over the years to rate his chances highly if he's forced to swim."

I'd grown up in San Francisco and was all too familiar with hazardous currents. "I don't know what we can do to help, but we've got to try. We can't stand here knowing Günter's out there alone."

My cousin appeared in the lobby, ashen-faced. "What's this about Günter?"

"His boat is sinking, and he's still on it," I said, getting straight to the point. "I'm heading to Carraig Harbour to see if I can help. Everyone else is focused on combating the flooding in Smuggler's Cove."

Lenny touched my arm. "I'll come with you, and we'll take my van. It's higher than Julie's MINI for driving in this weather."

In spite of the warmth of the lobby, my cousin wrapped her arms around her body. "How can we help Günter? I know you can sail, Lenny, but do you have access to a boat at Carraig Harbour? That's where Günter was keeping his houseboat, right?"

Lenny squared his shoulders. "I'm a lousy sailor, but if I can find a boat to take out, I'll give it my best shot."

"No need." Mary Driscoll appeared behind my cousin, flanked by her son and Mamie Byrne. "I'm a strong sailor, and so is Niall."

Niall was already pulling on his coat. "If Lenny deals with his chickens, I'll come with you now."

Relief flooded Lenny's face. "Thanks, mate. I'd probably sink the boat before I'd lifted the anchor."

In spite of the gloomy atmosphere, Lenny's brutal honesty made us all laugh.

"I keep a small fishing boat at Carraig Harbour," Niall continued. "Assuming my boat is still there, I'll try to get out to Günter. How fast is Günter's boat taking on water, Noreen?"

"Dickie Ahearn said he'd be good for an hour or so, but not much longer. And that's only if the boat doesn't capsize."

"I'll come, too," Mamie said. "I was a nurse before I opened the B&B."

I turned to Lenny and gave him a brief hug. "Good luck with the chickens."

"Be careful, Maggie. Don't underestimate the power of the ocean." My friend slipped a key out of his pocket. "Take my van. I'd feel more comfortable knowing you were higher up than in Julie's MINI."

I pocketed the key. "Thank you."

A few minutes later, I drove over roads that were slick with rainwater. Julie, Noreen, and Mamie had opted to come with me, while Niall and Mary Driscoll took his car. None of us was in the mood to talk, and I covered the distance from the Whisper Island Golf Club to Carraig Harbour in silence.

The instant after I'd pulled into a free spot in the harbor's parking lot, Julie rolled out of the car and ran to the side of the cliff. The rest of us hurried to catch up with her.

When my cousin looked at me, I read bleakness in her eyes. "I see Günter's boat. It's sinking fast."

The strong wind whipped the words out of her mouth, making it sound like she was far away instead of a foot in front of me.

I grabbed her arm. "Let's go down to the pier."

"What pier? The pier is completely submerged." Mamie came to my side, a pinched look on her weather-beaten face. "Niall will have to swim to reach his boat."

"Mamie's right. We're safer up here. Until Niall gets Günter to shore, there's nothing we can do."

I pulled my heavy raincoat tight around my body. "I hate feeling helpless. I came out here hoping I could assist with the rescue, but that's crazy talk."

"I feel the same, love." The rain had rendered Noreen's spectacles useless, so she'd removed them and was now blinking owlishly at the blurs around her.

"You raised the alarm," I said gently. "Well done."

"Do you think we should get back in the van?" Mamie's teeth chattered as she posed the question. "It's freezing out here."

Before answering, I surveyed my surroundings. My gaze settled on the whitewashed building next to the elevator. "The ferry office," I exclaimed in excitement. "They might have a radio in there. We could try to message the coast guard."

I was running before any of my companions had had a chance to react. As I'd expected, the office door was locked. I slipped my Swiss Army knife from my pocket. After a few minutes of fiddling, the lock gave way, and I burst inside. Mamie, Noreen, and Julie trooped in after me. Courtesy of the storm, the lights weren't working, but I found flashlights and a battery powered radio in a storage room and spent a frustrating fifteen minutes trying to coax the radio into life.

"Give up, love." Noreen bustled into the ticket office where I was working on the broken radio and handed me a mug of warm instant coffee.

I sniffed the mug, allowing the steam to warm my frozen face. "Where did you find a way to boil water?"

My aunt's smile was smug. "There's a portable gas cooker in that storage room you ransacked earlier. I figured if I couldn't do anything to help the rescue, I could at least make warm drinks for when everyone returns."

"Good thinking." I put the radio down and concentrated on my coffee. It tasted vile, but I needed the warmth offered by the hot liquid. "Where's Mamie? I wanted to ask her something."

"In the kitchen with Julie. Should I ask her to step in here?"

"Yes, please." If I couldn't contribute to Günter's rescue, I'd use the opportunity to talk to Mamie about her family's connection to the Malone brothers.

A moment later, Mamie came into the ticket office, clutching a mug in one hand, and perched on the stool opposite mine. She raised an eyebrow. "Noreen said you wanted a word with me."

"It's about something you said when Lenny and I visited Sergeant Reynolds at your B&B."

A flicker of unease passed over her lined features. "Oh, yes?"

"You mentioned that there were rumors about Mick Malone getting a girl pregnant. You took pains to add that you didn't know if that rumor was accurate."

Mamie jutted her jaw and fixed me with a defiant stare. "What of it? That was a long time ago."

"Was it a coincidence that you came into the golf club lobby at the same time as Mary Driscoll and her son? Because I got the impression that you and Mary were comfortable around one another, maybe even friends."

Mamie's stare didn't falter. "I have a lot of friends on Whisper Island. I've lived here my whole life."

"See, here's the thing: you and Mary are of a similar age. You must have gone to school at the same time. And Mary must have been a teenager when Niall was born. The guy's got to be around forty, and Mary can't be more than mid-fifties."

Finally, Mamie averted her gaze. "So?"

"So...is Mick Malone the father of Mary's son?"

The woman shrugged. "And what if he is? It's not as if the man was ever involved in Niall's life."

"The reason I ask is that the circumstance gives both Mary and Niall a strong motive to steal that necklace, and Mary works at the legal practice where it was stolen. It's not a stretch to imagine she could have discovered the combination to open the safe."

Mamie's eyes flashed with anger. "Mary would never do that. She's as honest as they come. And she needs that job. She'd never put her livelihood at risk to steal a necklace she wouldn't know how to sell."

"What about Niall? He strikes me as a clever sort. He could have stolen the necklace with the intention of selling it on the black market."

"Niall is my godson," Mamie said in an icy tone. "He would never do a thing like this."

"So you were deliberately vague about the details of the girl Mick Malone got pregnant."

She glared at me. "Mary is my best friend. She's stuck by me through all the ups and downs of my life. I'd never betray her. Mentioning the pregnancy to you was a mistake on my part."

"I have no intention of leading the police to an innocent person," I said, "but we both know Jennifer Pearce didn't take that necklace. She doesn't deserve to have her name dragged through the mud, and her professional reputation trashed."

Mamie's fists clenched at her sides. "Mary and Niall had nothing to do with the stolen necklace."

"What about you?" I asked softly. "Did you take the necklace to avenge the attack on your father?"

The woman jerked as if I'd struck her. "How did you find out about that?"

I didn't want to put Sergeant O'Mara in her line of fire, so I hedged. "The Whisper Island gossip mill has a long memory."

Mamie's eyes narrowed to slits, and her mouth trembled with rage. "I hate the Malones. It drives me crazy to see them staying in a fancy hotel like the Whisper Island Hotel and being feted like celebrities at the golf club."

"Did you take the necklace?" I repeated, keeping my voice steady.

"No." The word exploded from her, and then Mamie Byrne's ire appeared to deflate. "I can't stand the Malone brothers, but I have no beef with their sisters. I wouldn't want to jeopardize *their* inheritance."

Mamie sank onto the stool and stared unseeing into her mug.

"I'm sorry, Mamie, but I had to ask. Sergeant O'Shea has fixed on Jennifer as the culprit, and I don't trust him to look any farther."

The older woman snorted. "He's lazy, and Jennifer humiliated him during that murder case that you helped solve. O'Shea's perfectly happy to trash Jennifer's reputation."

"True." I sighed. "Unfortunately, none of this information brings me any closer to figuring out who stole the necklace."

"If you want, I can brainstorm with you," Mamie Byrne said in a gentler tone than she'd hitherto used during our fraught encounter.

"Let's go all out and ask Noreen and Julie if they want to help." I got to my feet. "It's either that or stress about how Günter's doing."

"I'll take the binoculars and look over the cliff to

see how the rescue is progressing. Meanwhile, get your aunt and cousin in here and we'll have a proper brainstorm when I return."

After Mamie had left, I asked Noreen and Julie to join us in the ticket office. Julie, a typical teacher, went in search of notepads and pens for all of us. We'd just finished getting everything ready for our brainstorming session when the door to the ticket office burst open. Mamie's reconnaissance hadn't taken long.

I glanced up, and my jaw dropped. Lenny stood on the threshold, rain running off his raincoat in rivulets. In his right hand, he lifted up a chicken cage containing a green-capped fowl. "Look what I found in Dooley's cage."

I frowned and took a step closer. And sucked in a breath. "Whoa. Is that—?"

"Yes." Lenny's bony face was agile with excitement. "Dooley is sitting on a diamond necklace."

12

I stared into the chicken's cage. Sure enough, Dooley the Runaway Chicken was perched atop a long, glittering necklace. I was no jewelry expert, but the diamonds looked like the real deal.

My eyes found Lenny's. "When did this happen?"

"I don't know. After you guys had left, I went back to the dressing room. I guess Niall had already gotten the chickens back in their travel coops. I didn't even notice the necklace at first because two of the chickens were fighting and had to be separated."

I suppressed a laugh at this image. "They were getting pretty restless once their performance was interrupted."

"Right." Lenny ran a hand through his scraggly brown hair. "They usually travel two to a coop, but Dooley and Donald were going for each other. Maybe they're into diamonds. Who knows? Anyway, while I was removing Donald from their shared coop, I noticed the necklace. Dooley won't let me anywhere near it. He goes nuts if I try."

I gave the chicken a wry smile. "Dooley has expensive tastes."

The chicken squawked as if to agree with my assessment.

Julie peered into the cage. "That must be the missing necklace that Jennifer is accused of stealing."

"Undoubtedly," Noreen said. "It's not like Whisper Island is swimming in millionaires."

"Speaking of swimming," I said, straightening, "how on earth did you get here? I took your van."

Lenny shot Julie a sheepish look. "I sort of hot-wired Julie's MINI."

My cousin opened and closed her mouth, fishlike. Finally, she said, "You never cease to amaze me, Lenny. I'm not sure which part shocks me most. The diamond necklace in the chicken coop or your misspent youth."

At that moment, the door swung open for the second time, and Mamie raced in, windblown and bedraggled. "I saw Niall and Mary pull Günter into their boat. There's no sign of his houseboat, so it looks like it sank faster than expected and Günter was forced to swim."

My cousin turned deathly pale. "Was he breathing?"

"I should say so. He swam to Niall's boat of his own accord."

Relief that matched my own flooded Julie's face. "Thank goodness."

"It's time for us to go out and help them." I looked around the room for confirmation. "They won't be able to use the elevator in this weather, so their only option is to climb the metal staircase."

Noreen shook her head. "Having us all hanging around on the edge of the cliff makes no sense. We'll take turns in keeping watch, divided into pairs. If they need help getting up the stairs, one of the watchers can run back and get the rest of us."

"There's rope in the storage room," I said. "I can take the first watch."

"No." Mamie patted my arm. "Stay here and do your thinking, Maggie. You can take your turn later."

"In that case, Julie and I will go out now," Noreen said. "Lenny, Mamie, and Maggie can brainstorm to their hearts' content. We'll come get you when we need you."

Over the next few minutes, we helped my aunt and cousin into their rain gear and provided them with rope and waterproof flashlights from the ticket office's emergency supplies room. After they'd left, Mamie, Lenny, and I armed ourselves with notepaper and pens and began our thinking session in earnest.

I went first. "So far, we've assumed that the theft of the necklace had two possible motives: financial gain and revenge. Under the financial gain list, we've put Mick and Enda Malone—Matt Malone's sons and two of his direct heirs. We've also added Matt and Enda's sons, Rob, Darren, and Brendan."

"And under the revenge list, we have Niall and Mary Driscoll and Mamie Byrne." Lenny pulled a face. "Sorry, Mamie, but we can't leave you off."

"I understand." The older woman chewed the end of her pencil, deep frown lines etched across her forehead. "You've mentioned the possibility that the thief took the necklace as revenge against the Malones, but what if they wanted to get revenge against Jennifer Pearce?"

"I considered that option early on," I said, "but I dismissed it pretty fast. When I spoke to Jennifer at length about her recent cases, she claims she can think of no reason why any of her clients—or anyone connected to her clients—would want revenge. She's a solicitor on a small island. She rarely deals with contentious matters, and an inheritance the size of Matt Malone's is rare. Ditto for her boss, Aaron Nesbitt. The one person with a grudge against Jennifer is Sergeant O'Shea. The man's an oaf, but I can't see him resorting to theft to avenge his humiliation."

Lenny nodded. "I agree. O'Shea's not a nice person, but he wouldn't break the law."

"Let's circle back to our original set of suspects." I scribbled names on my notepad, more to help me think than because I needed to jog my memory. "If one of the Malones took the necklace, he'd have had to discover the combination to the safe in Aaron and Jennifer's legal practice. The offices are protected by an alarm when the place is closed. So that person would have to be able to disable an alarm and crack a safe. Do any of the Malones have the tech know-how to do that?"

Lenny raised an eyebrow. "How about all of them? The elder Malone brothers make their living dealing in technical goods. Enda's catalog is enormous and almost certainly includes basic house alarms of the type installed at Nesbitt & Son. As for Mick, I know for a fact he carries them because my parents have his catalog."

"What about breaking into the safe?" Mamie's frown lines had softened somewhat, and she leaned forward, brimming with open curiosity. "Wouldn't that require expert knowledge?"

Lenny looked from one to the other of us. "Well, that's obvious, isn't it?"

Mamie and I exchanged a look of bewilderment.

"It is?" I shook my head. "Not to me."

"Ah, Maggie. *Think*. How could someone with no ability to crack a modern safe open it without being detected?"

I scrunched up my forehead. "Someone told them the code. But even if Mary Driscoll saw Aaron or Jennifer keying it in one day and memorized it, why would she inform the Malones? She might tell her son, though."

"No," Mamie said firmly. "Neither Mary nor Niall had anything to do with the theft of the necklace."

"What about Paddy Driscoll?" I persisted. "Perhaps he wanted to avenge his sister."

Lenny burst out laughing. "Paddy Driscoll is the type to punch a guy. I can't see him sneaking around breaking into safes. That's not Paddy's style at all."

"Then how could someone have discovered the code to the safe?" Before I'd finished voicing my question, the solution struck me. "Tech," I whispered. "Gadgets. The thief planted a camera in Aaron's office and filmed one of the lawyers opening the safe."

"Bingo." Lenny beamed at me. "That's what I suspect. Nanny cams are all the rage these days. If the thief used one of the more expensive models, the likelihood of Jennifer or Aaron noticing it is slim."

Mamie was practically bouncing up and down on her stool. "Whoever broke into the safe must have had access to the office."

"Apart from Mary, Aaron, and Jennifer, that opens the possibilities to cleaning staff and clients."

"Josie Mahon didn't do it," Mamie said decisively. "She cleans my B&B as well as Nesbitt & Son."

"Among Jennifer and Aaron's clients are the Malone brothers," I said. "Both Mick and Enda must have been in the office at some point to discuss their father's will."

"And if they contrived to get the office to themselves for a moment, it would have taken seconds to set up the camera." Lenny slapped his lap. "That's how they did it. Film the safe and monitor the feed on a computer. Once they'd captured the code, all they'd need to do is disable the alarm and open the safe."

"So it had to have been Mick or Enda?" I asked, my mind a whirl of information. "I don't mean to sound ageist, but the whole camera business sounds like a younger man's idea."

Lenny shrugged. "Mick and Enda sell computers and other electronic goods. We can assume they're pretty tech savvy. And why would their sons have been at Nesbitt and Co.? None of them are named in the will."

"True." *And yet...* A memory nagged at the back of my mind, a morsel of information that should be obvious to me but somehow remained on the periphery of my mental vision. My musings were cut short by a monumental crash. The door to the office burst open, and a shaking Günter staggered in, trembling violently.

Julie, Noreen, and the Driscolls followed, all wet and shivering.

I was on my feet in an instant. The next half hour passed in a flurry of boiling water for our wet friends and locating dry clothes for Günter. Clothes proved impossible to find, but there were several towels in the storage room, as well as a large overcoat of the type worn by janitors. Once Günter was dry, more or less clothed, and supplied with a hot beverage, we all settled in the ticket office to wait out the storm.

"You're a fool," Julie said to Günter, a hot flush staining her cheeks. "You could have drowned."

"That boat was my home," he replied, in a matter-of-fact tone. "I did what I could to save it."

My cousin glared at him. "And nearly drowned trying."

Günter grinned. "Nice to know you care, Julie."

I rolled my eyes. "I'm not sitting here all night listening to you two bicker. How about you help me crack a case?"

"Is this about the necklace?" The mention of the case had perked up Günter. "Any developments?"

"Oh, yeah." Lenny gestured to Dooley's cage. "The missing necklace is currently being guarded by a chicken."

Günter whistled. "Wow. Why would the thief put it in there?"

Niall frowned. "Are you serious? I didn't see any necklace when I got the chickens into their cages earlier."

"In other words, the necklace was put in the cage at some point between you coming into the lobby to offer your assistance in rescuing Günter and Lenny going back to the dressing room."

The older man blinked. "I guess so. I'd have noticed if that necklace had been in Dooley and Donald's cage for sure. It's huge and sparkly."

"Between the drama over the missing chicken and my dramatic fall from the stage, I lost track of who was in the audience for the chickens' dance and who left as part of the flood rescue group. What happened to all the Malones?"

"They all left except Mick." Mary's mouth formed a hard line. "I know because he came over to talk to me. I texted Niall to come and rescue me."

Her son picked up the tale from there. "That's why I was with Mum when Noreen came into the lobby with the news about Günter."

My heart rate kicked up a notch. "You're certain that Mick Malone was still in the auditorium when you left?"

Mary raised her head high. "Without a doubt."

"And his brothers, nephews, and son were not present?" I asked, pressing her to make sure I had my man.

"I'm positive they weren't there," Mamie said. "I was paying attention when Sergeant Reynolds divided the volunteers into groups. Enda, Rob, Darren, and Brendan were all assigned to various tasks. I overheard Brendan saying that his father was too drunk to be of any use."

"He stank of whiskey when he tried to talk to me." Mary wrinkled her nose in disgust. "It's funny. Enda was the one with the reputation as a heavy drinker back in the day."

"Forty years is a long time," I said. "People change."

Niall smirked. "In Mick's case, not enough. So am I right in assuming you think Mick stole the necklace?"

"I don't know. He's the one most likely to have put it in the chicken coop."

"But why?" Lenny demanded. "Why would he want to try to blame me?"

"I'm not sure he wanted to shift the blame onto you," I said to my friend. "I think he wanted that necklace to be found, and the chicken coop was such an unlikely place to stash it that the police wouldn't decide to blame you."

"Why would he want the necklace to be found?" Julie asked. I noticed that she'd moved a little closer to Günter, despite her grumpy treatment of him.

"Mick doesn't want Jennifer Pearce to be blamed for the theft. This way, the necklace will be handed over to the police, verified as authentic, and returned to the Malones."

"I don't understand," Mamie said, frowning.

Lenny my caught my eye. "But I do. When are you going to confront the culprit, Maggie?"

"As soon as the storm is over. In the meantime—" I removed the bottle of Jamesons I'd spotted in a desk earlier and placed it on the counter, "—does anyone want a hot toddy?"

13

The storm raged all night. We stayed in the ferry's ticket office until the wind and rain had dwindled to a brisk breeze and a smattering of rain drops. At eight o'clock the following morning, we judged it safe to venture outside.

"Do you want me to drop you home?" Lenny asked Noreen and me. "I could swing by your place on my way back to the Golf Club to collect the rest of the chickens."

"If you don't mind, I'd rather go straight to Smuggler's Cove and confront the thief. The sooner Jennifer's name is cleared, the better."

A wistful look spread over Lenny's long face. "Wish I could join you, but I need to get the chickens home to Granddad."

Julie laughed. "Seeing as we're hot-wiring one another's vehicles, take my MINI, Lenny. I'll drop everyone home and then collect the chickens from the golf club."

Our friend beamed. "Seriously? Thanks, dude."

After Lenny and Julie had exchanged keys, we all filed out of the ticket office. Niall and Mary Driscoll offered Günter a place to stay for the night, so he left in their car with Niall. Julie took Noreen and Mamie with her in the van, while Lenny, Mary, and I piled into Julie's MINI and headed to Smuggler's Cove. My phone finally had a signal, and I texted Sergeant Reynolds right away.

I know who stole the necklace. Where are you?

His response came almost instantly.

I'm at the school. All the volunteers are gathered here for soup and sandwiches, including Jennifer Pearce and Aaron Nesbitt.

"Head for the school." I settled back in the passenger seat and grinned at Lenny. "I feel like Hercule Poirot about to reveal his brilliance to a group of suspects."

My friend nodded to the backseat, where Dooley snoozed in his cage beside Mary. "By rights, we should thank Dooley for guarding the necklace with such ferocity."

Our progress to the school was slower than usual and delayed some more by an evidence gathering stop at Nesbitt & Son Solicitors. Mary let Lenny into the practice with her key. A few minutes later, they reappeared with triumphant expressions on their faces.

We continued our drive to the school. The road was strewn with branches. With the talent of a true islander, Lenny avoided all the flooded potholes and got us to the elementary school's parking lot unharmed.

"Ready?" he asked when we got out of the MINI.

I squared my shoulders. "As ready as I'll ever be."

Lenny grabbed Dooley's cage from the back, and we all ran toward the entrance.

As Reynolds had promised, everyone was gathered in the school's auditorium, seated on benches or fold-up chairs and eating soup. I scanned the crowd and spotted the Malones in a group. Mick had joined his family, presumably once he'd slept off the whiskey.

On the other side of the aisle, Jennifer was at a table with Aaron and her fiancé, Nick. She was making a valiant effort to ignore the Malones, but the rigid set of her shoulders told me harsh words had been exchanged.

I picked up my pace and strode toward them, coming to a halt between their respective groups. "Morning, folks. Time to get to the bottom of this necklace business, don't you think?"

Lenny obligingly held up Dooley's cage. The light streaming through the windows of the auditorium glinted off the diamond necklace. A gasp rippled through the crowd.

Enda Malone leaped to his feet. "Is that—?"

"Yes," I said before he could finish the thought. "Your brother was kind enough to stash it in the chicken's cage during last night's chaos. Isn't that right, Mick?"

Mick Malone paled. "I don't know what you're talking about."

Jennifer stood, her lips trembling. She pointed at Mick. "Did he steal the necklace and blame me?"

"No," I said without hesitation. "Mick found a way to return the necklace and clear your name."

The lawyer slow-blinked. "But why?"

"I think I can guess," a deep voice said.

I whirled around to see Sergeant Reynolds, arms crossed over his broad chest. His eyes met mine, and that familiar sizzle trailed down my spine.

"Why don't you tell them, Maggie?" he prompted. "You cracked the case after all."

"With help," I amended.

"Come on," Aaron Nesbitt demanded. "Who took the necklace from our safe? Who tried to frame Jennifer?"

I pivoted and fixed my gaze on the culprit. "Brendan Malone."

The young man flushed an angry red. "That's a lie. Why would I do that?"

"You stole the necklace to cover your gambling debts." My smile was brittle. "I'd imagine you've inherited your grandfather's love for poker, but not his business sense. Combined with lucrative sponsorship deals through golf, you've developed expensive tastes."

The young man's posture turned rigid. "You have no proof."

"Don't I?" I opened my palm to reveal the tiny camera that Lenny had placed in a sandwich bag to preserve fingerprints. Brendan's eyes darted toward the exit. I took a step closer, neatly blocking his escape route. "You asked your father to plant this camera in Aaron Nesbitt's office, possibly using the excuse that you didn't trust your uncle not to try to cheat your father out of his fair share of the inheritance. I don't know if Mick guessed your true purpose for wanting him to plant that camera, but he went along with it. Once your external feed had picked up a nice image of Aaron or Jennifer keying in the code to open the safe, you broke into the office one night and snatched a necklace. I'm not sure why you didn't take all four, but perhaps some small part of your conscience prevented you from taking all your grandfather had bequeathed his children."

Brendan's Adam's apple bobbed. "You can't prove any of this."

I shrugged. "Let's see if you're still singing that tune when your DNA is found at Nesbitt & Son, a place you've allegedly never entered."

In truth, I had no idea if Brendan's DNA was on the premises, but I wanted to make the guy sweat. Judging by the sheen of perspiration on his upper lip, I was succeeding.

"Dad, do something." Brendan's voice was a whine.

Mick Malone stared at his feet. "I've done too much already, son."

"And I've heard enough to take both of you in for questioning." Reynolds moved forward and grabbed Brendan's arm. "I'm not charging you with a crime yet, but I strongly recommend you engage a solicitor."

Lenny snorted. "That'll take a while. Aaron and Jennifer are the only solicitors on Whisper Island, and I don't see them agreeing to represent this pair."

Jennifer placed her hands on her hips. "As far as I'm concerned, they can both rot in a cell until they find someone to come over to the island. I'm done with the Malones as clients."

"I second Jennifer." Aaron got to his feet, an angry flush across his pale cheeks. "I'll make immediate arrangements to engage another solicitor to handle Matt Malone's estate."

Sergeant Reynolds escorted a protesting Brendan Malone outside to his squad car, trailed by a shamefaced Mick Malone. Once both men had been secured in the back of the police vehicle, Sergeant Reynolds turned his bright blue eyes on me. "Well done, Maggie."

To my embarrassment, my cheeks grew warm. "No problem. As I said, I had a lot of help along the way."

His amused smile left me flustered. "But you were the one who untangled all the threads. That takes a rare talent."

For a long moment, my words caught in my throat.

"I like solving puzzles," I said finally, kicking myself for my lame response. "And I don't like innocent people being accused of stuff they didn't do."

The police sergeant gave me a mock salute. "Good work. But can we make a deal?"

"Sure." My chest swelled. He was going to ask me out on a date. I could sense it. But what would I say when he did?

His lips began to move, but it took a moment to comprehend what he was saying. "From now on, leave the detecting to me."

My happy smile reversed in time to register my nails digging into my palms. "You're warning me off your territory?"

Sergeant Reynolds' smile was conciliatory. "I wouldn't quite put it like that. I'm merely pointing out that Whisper Island will soon have a competent police officer in charge of future investigations, and you don't have a private investigator's license."

I pulled back my shoulders and shot him my dirtiest look. "And what if I got one?"

His laugh was half amused, half regretful. "You're only in Ireland for a couple more months, Maggie. Why don't you do what you came here to do? Relax and forget about real life stresses. You deserve a break."

With as much dignity as I could muster with my rain-sodden hair, I tossed frizzy curls over my shoulder and lifted my chin in defiance. "If you think you'll get rid of me that easily, you have another think coming,

Sergeant. If I see a wrong that needs to be put right, I'll do it, license or no license."

He threw his head back and laughed, the hearty sound whipping around my ears in the wind. "How did I know you'd say that?"

On instinct, I flipped him the bird, changing it into a peace sign at the last second. Indignant and fuming, I turned on my heel and marched down the road, destination unknown. Reynolds' laughter rang in my ears for a long time.

∽

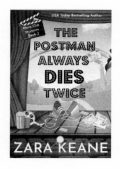

Thanks for reading *To Hatch a Thief*. I hope you enjoyed Maggie's latest adventure!

The Movie Club Mysteries continue in **The Postman Always Dies Twice**.

Breathing hard, I gave a yelp and let the now-empty canister drop to the ground. "That wasn't pepper spray." I stared into the sparkly, green face of the corpse I'd discovered mere hours before. "And you're not dead."

When Maggie extends her stay in Ireland, dealing with more murder and mayhem isn't on her to-do list. The instant she discovers the dead body of the

Whisper Island postman, her plan to chill for the next two months is put on ice. Can Maggie solve the crime before St. Patrick's Day? Or will the island's annual parade come to a deadly end? **Find out now!**

If you'd like to get up to date with the Movie Club Mysteries, and get a **FREE** story, **join my mailing list. Sign up at zarakeane.com/movieclubmysteriesnewsletter/**

Happy Reading!
Zara xx

Join my mailing list and get news, giveaways, and free stories!

Sign up on zarakeane.com/movieclubmys-teriesnewsletter

Would you like to try one of the cocktails Maggie made for the *To Catch a Thief* movie night? There are a few variations on this classic cocktail that gained popularity in 1920s Paris. Here's Maggie's favorite combo!

ROSE COCKTAIL

- 2 oz (60ml) dry vermouth
- 1 oz (30ml) Kirschwasser
- 1 tsp raspberry syrup or Chambord

1. Put all the ingredients into a cocktail shaker.
2. Add ice and shake vigorously.
3. Strain into a chilled cocktail glass.

Maggie's tip: If you're serving a series of gin-based cocktails, you can easily add 1oz dry gin, and lower the amount of dry vermouth from 2oz to 1 oz.

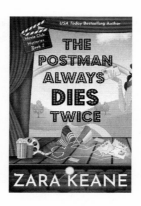

The Movie Club Mysteries continue in *The Postman Always Dies Twice.*

When former San Francisco cop, Maggie Doyle, extends her stay in Ireland, dealing with more murder and mayhem isn't on her to-do list. The instant Maggie and her UFO-enthusiast friend discover the dead body of the Whisper Island postman, Maggie's plans to chill for the next two months are put on ice.

After Police Sergeant Reynolds, Maggie's handsome neighbor, arrests Lenny's brother for the murder, her friend begs her to find the real killer. Meanwhile, Maggie is hired to investigate ghostly goings on at the Whisper Island Hotel. Can she solve two crimes before St. Patrick's Day? Or will the island's annual celebrations end in a glittery flame of green, white, and orange?

EXCERPT FROM *THE POSTMAN ALWAYS DIES TWICE*

Whisper Island, Ireland

I'd encountered plenty of culture shocks since I'd swapped my cheating husband and my career in the San Francisco PD for a remote Irish island. Discovering that used car salesmen were the same slick, sons-of-guns all over the world was almost a comfort.

I fixed the proprietor of Zippy Motors with a hard stare. "I'll give you three hundred bucks, and not a penny more."

"Aw, come on, Maggie. A man's gotta eat. This little beauty will zip you around—just like our slogan." Jack Logan treated me to the killer smile that had left a trail of broken hearts across Whisper Island in the years before he'd developed a beer belly and a comb-over. I remained unmoved.

"The car's fit for scrap metal," I said. "Before I shell out any money, never mind your insane asking price, I need to know the vehicle will survive the couple of months I'm staying on the island."

"Sure it will." Jack spread his palms wide in a gesture that was presumably designed to put his customers at ease. "Would I sell you a lemon? I value my reputation."

I rolled my eyes. "Your reputation stinks. You're

still in business because you get an influx of clueless tourists every summer who are willing to rent one of your wrecks for the season."

The salesman's composure faltered. "Now that's a bit harsh."

"But true. I'm Lenny's friend, remember? Your cousin's told me all about you." And the parts Lenny hadn't told me, I could guess. Jack wore designer clothes and reeked of expensive aftershave. I glanced up at Zippy Motors's battered sign. Somehow, I doubted Jack funded his flash lifestyle with the money he made from selling and renting wrecks.

I strolled around the Ford Fiesta, examining it for obvious patches of rust. "Today's your lucky day, Jack. I'm in need of a cheap ride, and your establishment is on the island if there's any trouble with my purchase." I made eye contact. "You do offer an after purchase warranty, right?"

The man's Adam's apple bobbed. "Uh, sure, but nothing will go wrong with the car."

"For your sake, I hope not." I patted the ancient vehicle and it didn't fall apart under my touch. I took this to be a good sign. "Cash, I presume?"

After I'd completed my transaction with Jack Logan, I slid behind the wheel of my new-to-me ride and drove out of Smuggler's Cove. I hung a left at the crossroads on the edge of town, and headed in the direction of my new home—a sweet little holiday cottage on the far side of Whisper Island. As a Thank

You for my help in solving a murder mystery, my aunts and friends had pooled their resources to pay for two months' rent on the cottage, thus treating me to an extended vacation on their island. I'd moved in last week. After spending six weeks living with my aunt, Noreen, and her menagerie of animals, I was still getting used to the silence.

The drive across the island took thirty minutes. I took it slow, soaking in the sights. The snow we'd had earlier in the winter hadn't lasted long, and now that it was early March, the first signs of spring were starting to show. The days were growing longer, and a few flowers had begun to bloom. As the road wound around the edge of the cliffs, I passed woodland and rolling green hills before finally reaching the gates of my new residence.

My cottage was part of a complex of eight holiday homes named Shamrock Cottages—although I had yet to see any evidence that shamrocks grew in the vicinity. Built on a slope, the cottage boasted a spectacular view of the sea through my front windows. Each cottage in the complex had a fenced-in garden with just enough room for an outdoor table and chairs. There was also a communal playground, as well as a shared games room.

When I drove through the gates of Shamrock Cottages, my aunt, Noreen, was waiting on my doorstep. She wore a wide smile on her face, and balanced a tray of freshly baked scones in her arms. My mouth watered at the sight. Since moving out of her house, I'd started to skip breakfast. Not smart, but it had helped me lose a few of the pounds I'd gained while living with Noreen and eating her enormous portions. Bran, my aunt's lively Border collie-Labrador mix, danced by her side, tripping over Noreen's large bag in his excitement to see me.

The instant I stepped out of my car, Bran bounded over and treated me to an obligatory crotch sniff. "Cut that out," I said, bending down to pet his soft fur. "You gotta learn manners."

"Too late for that, I'm afraid," my aunt said with a laugh. "I've tried everything. On the plus side, he only does it to people he likes."

I scratched Bran under his chin. "While I'm honored to be liked by you, Bran, I wish you'd show your affection for me in some other way."

As if he understood my words, the dog treated my hand to a generous lick. I gave him a last pat and drew my key from my jacket pocket.

My aunt squinted at the car and then leaped back in horror. "Please don't tell me you went to Zippy Motors."

"They're cheap, and I'm low on cash." I slammed the driver's door and strode toward the cottage door, Bran at my heels. "Mmm. Those scones smell divine."

My aunt clucked with disapproval. "Don't change the subject. Jack Logan is a snake. I buy cheap cars, but even I won't go near him. I'm convinced he's laundering money at that place."

"It's a done deal now," I said cheerfully. I unlocked the door and relieved my aunt of the tray. "Want to come in for a coffee? Because I'm totally eating one of these scones."

"That would be lovely." My aunt bounded into the cottage with an agility that belied her fifty-six years. "I have some housewarming gifts for you."

I raised an eyebrow. "More? You've already given me enough towels to dry a family of six."

Noreen bounced on the spot, making her jet-black curls dance. "These gifts are of a more lively nature. Literally."

I sucked in a breath. "Oh, no. Not the pet thing again."

"Just hear me out before you object, Maggie. You could do with some company now that you're out here all alone. Bran can act as a guard dog."

I placed the tray on the kitchen counter and shook my head emphatically. "You're not foisting the dog onto me. No way. Besides, I live next door to a policeman. What could be safer than that?"

My aunt clucked in disapproval. "Sure, Sergeant Reynolds hasn't moved in properly yet. Even if he had, he'd hardly ever be home. He's working crazy hours in pursuit of those eejits who keep sneaking onto farms and causing havoc. Did you hear about Paddy Driscoll's sheep?"

"Clearly, I'm behind on island gossip." I switched

on the coffee machine and got out plates and coffee mugs. "What happened to Paddy's sheep?"

"They were given a makeover last night,"

I looked at my aunt over my shoulder and slow-blinked. "What does a sheep makeover involve?"

"They were dressed in knitted outfits made out of acrylic yarn."

"Wow." I whistled. "An animal activist on a mission?"

"Maybe. At any rate, Paddy's chief issue was the fact that the pattern on the sheeps' outfits was the Union Jack." Noreen's lips twitched with amusement. "Not a flag likely to please a man of Paddy's political persuasions."

I recalled the huge Irish flag painted on the wall of Paddy's barn, and the various pro-I.R.A. sentiments the grumpy farmer had uttered in my presence. No, he wouldn't be pleased to find his sheep wearing the British flag.

After I'd made a cappuccino for my aunt and a double espresso for me, I placed two of the scones on plates and put everything on the table. On autopilot, I retrieved one of the doggie snacks I kept for Bran's visits from the drawer under the sink.

"I'm serious about you adopting Bran," my aunt said, watching me feed the grateful dog his treat. "You're the one taking him on most of his walks these days.

"It's not fair to the dog. I'm only on Whisper Island until May."

"Until the end of May," my aunt corrected, as though the distinction made all the difference in the world. "Why don't you take him until then? He'll be great company for you and the cats."

"Cats?" My voice rose in a crescendo. I sucked in a breath and scanned the kitchen for evidence of feline habitation. My gaze came to rest on the big carrier bag at Noreen's feet and I groaned out loud. "Oh, no."

Inside the carrier bag, six kittens snuggled against their mother, snoozing peacefully in a basket.

"Seeing as you rescued Poly's kittens, I thought you'd like to have a couple of them to keep you company. They're not ready to leave their mum permanently yet, so I brought her with them."

"A couple doesn't mean six. Besides, Sergeant Reynolds rescued one of the kittens. I just helped."

"Exactly." My aunt beamed at me. "Rosie is the one on the far left. I'm sure she'd love to come and live with you."

"Not happening, Noreen. I love you to bits, but the animals are leaving when you do."

My aunt grinned across the table and spread a generous helping of strawberry jam over her scone. "I'll wear you down, Miss Maggie. You just see if I don't."

Before I could utter another protest, the familiar splutter of an old VW van drew my attention to the kitchen window. Through the glass, I saw my friend,

Lenny, park his van at the entrance to Shamrock Cottages. Like my car, the van had seen better years, and better paint jobs. Lenny's recent decision to paint it psychedelic purple hadn't enhanced the vehicle's appeal.

"Lenny just pulled up," I told my aunt. "I'll go let him in."

When I opened my front door, Lenny was ambling toward me, carrying a large plastic bag. He stopped short when he saw my new car and circled it as one would a feral beast. "Aw, Maggie. You went to Jack's place? What did I tell you about that guy?"

"That he's a crook and a swindler and to run far and fast," I replied. "And although Jack's cons list outweighs his pros, he's cheap and easily intimidated."

"I wouldn't be so sure about the easily intimidated part," Lenny said, tugging on his scraggly beard. "He's bold enough to drive a brand new Porsche around the island one minute, and plead poverty to the Inland Revenue the next."

"I take it Jack isn't keen on paying taxes?"

"That's one way of putting it. But enough about my idiot cousin. How are you doing? All settled into your new home?" My friend's easy-going smile lit up his thin face, transforming him from homely to kinda-cute-in-a-geeky-sorta-way. We'd been buddies since I'd spent my summers on Whisper Island as a child. Although we'd lost touch as adults, our friendship had picked up where we'd left off when I returned to the island in January.

"It's fab. I like it so much it'll be hard to leave when the lease is up." I nodded in the direction of the kitchen. "Want to come in for a coffee? Noreen's here and she brought scones."

"I can't stay. I have to go to Paddy Driscoll's place to fix his computer." He held up the plastic carrier bag. "I thought I'd swing by yours on the way and give you your housewarming present."

"As long as it's not a pet, we're good," I quipped, remembering the basket of kittens with a sinking sensation in my stomach. I had a feeling Noreen would wear me down.

"No worries." Lenny's bony face split into a grin that brought a twinkle to his pale blue eyes. "I thought you needed a little greenery in your new home."

He opened the bag and removed a leafy potted plant...a leafy potted cannabis plant. "I thought it'd liven up your new home."

"I can think of more legal ways to liven up my cottage." I shot him a look of exasperation. "Have you forgotten I live next door to a police officer?"

Lenny's grin faded. "Oops. I didn't think of Reynolds."

"You don't say," I said, deadpan. "Even if I was inclined to keep it, I have an unfortunate track record with plants.

Bran and my aunt emerged from the kitchen.

"She's not joking," Noreen said, pulling on her coat. "She killed a cactus while she was staying with me."

I grimaced. "Guilty as charged."

When she'd buttoned up her duffel coat, Noreen squeezed my arm. "I'd best be off, love. I need to get to the café and relieve Fiona. I'll collect you at six-thirty for the Movie Club meeting. Will that suit you?"

"Six-thirty sounds good." I noticed a conspicuous absence of kittens in her carrier bag. "Whoa. You're not leaving me with the cats and—" Bran rubbed against my legs, silencing me with the plaintive expression in his doggie eyes. I bit back a sigh. Who could resist that look? "Do you want to stay with me for a while, buddy?"

Bran's response was to lick my hand. Man, that dog knew how to pull at my heartstrings.

"If you're keeping Bran, you can hardly turf out the cats," Noreen said as if the matter was decided. She paused when she noticed the plant in my arms. "Oh, that's a beautiful bit of greenery."

I laughed. "A beautiful bit of greenery that's destined for the garbage can."

"Oh, no." My aunt looked horrified. "You can't do that. I'll take it home with me."

"Noreen, that's not a good idea."

"It'd look great in your house," Lenny said straight-faced. "It'd definitely add class to the joint."

I shot him a warning look. "Don't listen to him. Take my advice and get rid of it."

"Nonsense," Noreen said. "I have loads of plants. It'll fit right in."

I opened my mouth to protest, but my words were drowned out by the roar of a motorcycle crunching up the gravel drive. Sergeant Liam Reynolds pulled up outside his cottage, and leaped off his bike. He pulled off his helmet to reveal close-cropped dark blond hair and a face that would have been movie star handsome but for a nose that had been broken more than once. To my annoyance, a jolt of desire set my blood humming.

"Uh, oh," Lenny whispered beside me. "Now we're for it."

The words I muttered beneath my breath were less polite. "What possessed you to show up here with a cannabis plant?" I whispered.

"I'm sorry," Lenny whispered back. "I thought it would give you a laugh."

Reynolds, also known as Sergeant Hottie—okay, known as Sergeant Hottie *by me*—pulled off his helmet and smiled at us. My heart thumped a little faster.

"Coo-ee," my aunt called. To my horror, she held up the cannabis plant for Reynolds to see. "Look what Maggie gave me. Isn't it lovely?"

Oblivious to the policeman's slack-jawed expression, my aunt got into her car, waved to us, and drove off with the cannabis plant on her passenger seat.

Want more? *The Postman Always Dies Twice* is available on all major book stores.

ABOUT THE AUTHOR

USA Today bestselling author Zara Keane grew up in Dublin, Ireland, but spent her summers in a small town very similar to the fictitious Whisper Island and Ballybeg.

She currently lives in Switzerland with her family. When she's not writing, Zara loves knitting, running, unplugged gaming, and adding to her insanely large lipstick collection.

Zara has an active Facebook reader group, **Zara Keane's Mystery Mavens**, where she chats, shares snippets of upcoming stories, and hosts members-only giveaways. She hopes to join you for a virtual pint very soon!

zarakeane.com

Made in United States
North Haven, CT
15 February 2023

32634781R00088